Barrabas h[...]
when his le[...]

There was no time t[...]

At the sound of the sn[...] he reacted, jerking to one side, bringing his forearms up. The blow delivered by the spring of green bamboo knocked him flat on his butt. It would have broken a smaller man's arms. He looked up at the spiked head of the bamboo whip, his heart pounding. Had he moved the other way, the cluster of fire-hardened bamboo spines would have skewered him like a fondue tidbit.

Then he heard the bell attached to the booby trap. The signal had been sprung.

Barrabas stared into the bush—and tried not to think about dying.

MAP OF
SON NY'S DEFENSES

MINED AREA

EXITS TO
ABOVE GROUND

TO AMBUSH SITE

MG

MG

ARMORED MACHINE-GUN EMPLACEMENTS

COVERED TRENCHES/TUNNELS (GROUND LEVEL)

PLANTATION HOUSE

FRONT

MG

MG

MAXIMUM ARC OF FIRE (ESTIMATED)

MINED AREA

RUBBER-TREE GROVES

DIRT TRACK TO MATALE ROAD

SOBs

BUTCHERS
OF EDEN

JACK HILD

A GOLD EAGLE BOOK FROM
W*RLDWIDE

TORONTO • NEW YORK • LONDON • PARIS
AMSTERDAM • STOCKHOLM • HAMBURG
ATHENS • MILAN • TOKYO • SYDNEY

First edition November 1984

ISBN 0-373-61603-1

Special thanks and acknowledgment to
Alan Philipson for his contributions to this work.

Copyright © 1984 by Worldwide Library.
Philippine copyright 1984. Australian copyright 1984.

All rights reserved. Except for use in any review, the
reproduction or utilization of this work in whole or in part
in any form by any electronic, mechanical or other means,
now known or hereafter invented, including xerography,
photocopying and recording, or in any information storage
or retrieval system, is forbidden without the permission
of the publisher, Worldwide Library, 225 Duncan Mill Road,
Don Mills, Ontario, Canada M3B 3K9. All the characters in
this book have no existence outside the imagination of the
author and have no relation whatsoever to anyone bearing the
same name or names. They are not even distantly inspired by
any individual known or unknown to the author, and all the
incidents are pure invention.

The Gold Eagle trademark, consisting of the words
GOLD EAGLE and the portrayal of an eagle, and the
Worldwide trademark, consisting of the word
WORLDWIDE in which the letter ''O'' is represented by a
depiction of a globe, are trademarks of Worldwide Library.

Printed in Canada

1

Karl Heiss clapped his palms over his ears, pressing until he thought his skull would crack. Still he could not shut out the sounds from the courtyard.

The shouted commands in Swahili.

The firing squad's deafening chorus.

He could not shut out the sound of laughter, either. Laughter from the other side of his prison cell. Across from Heiss squatted a man also fettered by ankle chains running through a locked steel hasp set in the concrete floor. Defeated, Heiss lowered his trembling hands.

"And I thought you ex-CIA boys ate nails three times a day," his grinning cellmate said.

"Shut up!" Heiss snarled back.

The man continued to grin. "Easy, friend," he said, "our hosts are just playing games with us. They didn't execute anybody out there. They couldn't have. I heard some guards talking this morning when they brought me in. There's no one left for them to shoot but you and me."

Heiss glanced over his shoulder at the barred window set high in the filth-spattered wall, but made no move to get up from the floor. Even if he had cared to, he could not test the Belgian mercenary's theory. With chains and body stretched to the limit, he could barely touch the bottom of the sill with his fingertips.

"Face it. They're saving us," the man went on. "We're trophies of the great Kaluban war of democratic freedom. They've got to have some white faces to drag through the streets on national holidays. Foreign gangsters for the mob to throw garbage at."

Heiss glared at the Belgian and said nothing. Newly captured, the smug bastard had no idea how the Kalubans ran their detention camps. He had no concept of the games they played with their prisoners, either. For three months, while Karl Heiss was experiencing the African island nation's penal system firsthand, the mercenary had been out in the jungle, living off the land, eluding the armed forces loyal to the government. It was dumb luck that the man had escaped to begin with. He had been in the right place—out in the field—when the attempted coup by Field Marshall Haile Mogabe was blocked. Heiss, on the other hand, had been stuck at the airport in the capital, trapped while trying to make the last flight out before the borders were sealed.

Ninety days in the bush had been kind to the Belgian merc. He was perfectly sound in mind and body. After ninety days in prison the same could not be said of Karl Heiss.

With a resounding clank the cell-block door opened.

Heiss went rigid, then panicked. He tried desperately to hurl himself into a far corner, but his chains would not allow it. He curled into a fetal ball on the concrete and buried his head beneath his arms. Over the Belgian's laughter he could hear hobnailed boots quick-marching down the corridor toward them. Then a key rattled in the lock of the cell door. He curled tighter when the door swung back. The officer in charge of the execution squad made his announcement in English. Heiss already knew it by heart.

"By order of the Provisional Judiciary Council of the Democratic Republic of Kaluba, for war crimes and atrocities committed against the nation and its people, you have been condemned to death by firing squad. The sentence will be carried out at once."

Padlocks were quickly opened and the prisoners' ankle chains removed from the hasps. A pair of black soldiers jerked Heiss to his feet. For an instant he was held almost nose to nose with his Belgian counterpart, who apparently no longer found the proceedings amusing. The man's face was full of anger, not fear, his eyes hard focused, their gaze level. Then the mercenary was shoved out into the corridor. Without prodding, he began to hobble along between an escort of khaki-uniformed executioners, his head erect, defiant.

"Now, there's a man who knows how to die," the squad leader said.

Heiss shuddered. The squad leader was smiling at

him, dimpled ebony cheeks gleaming with oil and sweat. They were all smiling at him. Heiss, too, had walked out under his own power.

The first time.

Then came the bum's rush. Sudden. Startling. To minimize struggle. The black soldiers seized him by the upper arms and carried him out the cell door. They dragged him screaming and thrashing down the corridor, past a gauntlet of furious black faces inside dank cells. Black hands clawed for him between iron bars. It was a gauntlet of curses and spit. Half starved for months, Heiss was no match for the men who hauled him along. In seconds he exhausted himself. He was pulled weeping from the cell block, out into the soft golden light of sunset.

Above the high, plastered brick outer wall of the compound, the feathery tops of palm trees hung dead still. The sweltering air seethed with insect song and swooping bats. Heiss was blind to everything but the rut beneath his feet. The track, dredged out of the cinder and packed dirt of the courtyard by the heavy links of chain that joined the ankles of the doomed, marked the shortest route between the cell-block door and the place of execution.

The Belgian was already backed up against the wall, his hands pulled behind him and secured. He puffed his chest out, held his chin high and regarded the cringing Heiss with contempt.

Appearances had long ceased to matter to Karl Heiss.

The soldiers shoved him face first against the bullet-pocked wall and pinned him there. His cheek grated on the rough plaster while a third soldier deftly joined his thumbs together with figure eights of steel wire. The Belgian was right. Their jailers had been toying with them this evening. There was no evidence of a previous execution, no corpses strewn about. And the plaster against his cheek was bone dry.

They twisted Heiss face front and left him leaning against the wall. His knees were so weak he could not have stood without its support. He watched dry mouthed as the six-man firing squad picked up their weapons, battered and worn FN FALs. They joked in Swahili as they formed a ragged line thirty feet away.

The officer in charge stepped up to the Belgian and without a word pulled a black cloth hood down over the man's head. Under the hood the mercenary began muttering prayers or curses; it was impossible to tell which.

Then it was Heiss's turn.

The squad leader raised a hood over his head.

"No, please," Heiss said in a hoarse whisper. "Please don't."

The hood came down, blotting out the light. It had been used many times before. The cloth was no longer soft. It was stiff, encrusted. The feel of it on his face, its stench, paralyzed him. In darkness he was utterly alone, abandoned. Not that he had seriously thought his partner in the Mogabe deal would attempt to rescue him. At last word, Simon Brookler was safe in Amsterdam with both their shares of the diamonds.

A hand gripped his shoulder, and the officer spoke softly into his ear. "This time you die," he said. The officer's boot heels crunched on the cinders as he took a step to the side. Then he called his men to attention.

Heiss's heart was hammering, hard, fast; it felt as if it was about to explode. Like a lost child he began to whimper.

During his imprisonment, Karl Heiss had faced a Kaluban firing squad three times before. Three times he had stood with his thumbs wired together behind his back, the stinking hood over his head, listening as an officer's commands counted down the last seconds of his life. Three times battle rifles had cracked, dropping prisoners on either side of him, while Heiss stood quivering, awaiting the lethal impact that never came.

Beside him now, the Belgian's mumblings grew louder and much more distinct. They were prayers in French, spoken in a clear, steady voice. The mercenary was showing the depth of his courage while Heiss sniveled and choked.

Facing execution once with dignity was no great feat.

Heiss had done it, too.

The apparent certainty of death that first time had made it easy for him to prepare a noble exit. He had had nothing to lose. After that, everything changed. A hope of survival, of a last-second reprieve, however slim, corroded his will and devoured him from within. Despite what the officer had just told him, Heiss clung to the faint hope that what had happened before might happen again; he clung like the proverbial drowning man.

"Ready!" the squad leader said.

There was a dry clatter as rifles were cocked.

"Aim!"

At that terrible, final instant, hope slipped through Heiss's grasp. And his thoughts were only of the man with the white hair. The man who had brought down the murderous revolutionary cadre Heiss had been part of. The man who, by stranding Heiss at the Tomalave airport, had in effect put him hard against the execution wall four times. "Goddamn you, Nile Barrabas!" he sobbed. "Damn you to hell!"

FALs roared. And this time Karl Heiss was struck. A terrible blow over his heart. The impact hurled him back into the wall and sent him sprawling forward to the ground on his face. He lay there, gasping, writhing from the pain in the center of his chest.

Through the hood he heard the quick crunch of boots on cinder. Then the flat whack of a handgun as the squad leader administered the *coup de grâce* to the Belgian.

It was coming. An end to the pain. An end to everything.

With the toe of his boot the officer rolled Heiss

over onto his back. He bent down and jerked the
hood from the prisoner's head. Heiss blinked up at
the broad silhouette against a blood-red sky. The
officer transferred the automatic pistol to his left
hand.

"Finish it," Heiss groaned. "For God's sake,
finish it!"

There were muffled guffaws from the firing
squad.

"Get up!" the officer said.

Heiss did not move.

"Up!" the squad leader repeated, threatening
Heiss with a clenched right fist. "Get up or I'll hit
you again."

Understanding struck Heiss like a second punch
over his heart, this one in slow motion. He was not
shot. He was not dying. It was another round of the
same twisted game. Overwhelmed by fury and terror and his own helplessness in the face of both,
Heiss fell into a violent, shivering fit.

Nothing could stop the laughter of the firing
squad then. They hooted, they howled, clutching at
their stomachs, slapping their thighs as they pointed
at him.

Heiss shut his eyes and ears to them, his mind
turning in on itself to keep from being torn apart.

The officer let his men have their fun for a
minute or two, then brought them back under control with a sharp command. "Pick him up and take
him to his cell."

Heiss did not struggle as he was hauled back to

the cell block. Focusing his impotent rage on a fantasy of revenge, he was only dimly aware of what was happening. Inside his head, Heiss had the man with the white hair strapped to a straight-backed chair while he hacked two-handed with a razor-honed machete, hacked and hacked until there was no face, no skull, only a red knob of spine jutting up from between blood-bathed shoulders.

The mingled odors of a steaming human zoo jolted Heiss back to the world of the real. On the other side of the iron bars, black faces were no longer furious; they were beaming, glad to see him alive, glad because his torments were not ended yet. His fellow inmates were domestic criminals, thieves, murderers, deviates. There was no bullet-pocked wall in their future, no quick exit from the hunger, disease and brutality that were integral parts of a prison sentence on the African island. As a symbol, Karl Heiss stirred the patriotic outrage of even these lowliest of Kalubans. He was the white exploiter, the profiteer in armaments. With his guns and his ammunition the revolutionary army of Haile Mogabe had slaughtered thousands of noncombatants, innocent citizens.

The soldiers dumped Heiss onto the floor of his cell, locked his ankle chains through the hasp and left. It was already dark outside; it was never dark inside. A diesel generator growled twenty-fours hours a day, keeping alight the string of bare bulbs that dangled from the corridor ceiling.

Slowly, stiffly, Heiss drew himself up into a sitting position. He was already falling apart, and the evening's unpleasantness had only just begun. If past experience was any guide, soon another squad of soldiers would unlock his chains and take him to the prison interrogator for an all-night grilling on the CIA's current objectives in Kaluba, a subject he knew nothing about. Though he had done his damnedest, he had been unable to convince his captors that he was no longer on the CIA's mailing list, only on its Most Wanted list. At first their preoccupation seemed to be typical Third World paranoia; they saw the hand of American intelligence in every chicken that dropped dead by the side of the road. And it *was* common knowledge that the CIA had provided the initial funding for the Mogabe revolutionaries, only to withdraw its support when Mogabe himself could not be controlled.

Of late other, grimmer possibilities had begun to haunt Heiss. Perhaps the Kalubans' aim was not to gather information but to destroy him, to pound on his psyche until it shattered. They were certainly stupid enough to believe that a broken ex-CIA op might be of some value in future U.S. negotiations. Or, perhaps even simpler, it was all merely part of his punishment, a way for the government to squeeze maximum agony—and retribution—from his death sentence.

Losing was something Karl Heiss looked at philosophically, as an inevitable corollary of the law of averages. Facing justice was another story. Heiss always considered himself a superior man, above the rules and penalties of others. Above the rules of Harvard, where he had cheated his way through undergraduate school. Above the rules of the U.S. State Department, too. Degree in fist, he had snow-jobbed his way into the foreign service, then through blackmail had wrangled himself a much prized post in the Saigon mission. The year was 1968. As one of the second secretaries to the economics minister, he was low man in the bureaucratic order of things. Heiss cared nothing about his position on that ladder. He was in Saigon to make personal contact with Vietnamese bankers, manufacturers, military leaders and black marketeers, to help himself to some of the cream, the surpluses and wastes of a distant and unpopular war.

He found his element in Vietnam. It was chaos. In a place of danger, doubt and fear, with the protections of diplomatic immunity, Karl Heiss came into his own.

It was also there that Heiss met the man who would become his nemesis. The man with the white hair.

Heiss despised Nile Barrabas long before he ever set eyes on him. Saigon of the late sixties was a small pond, and the then Major Barrabas a big fish. A genuine American war hero. A rugged and uncompromising leader of men. After Barrabas's posting to MACV (Pentagon East) it was rare to open the social page of *Stars and Stripes* without seeing his name two or three times, his presence noted at such and such a party in the company of a general's daughter, a diplomat's niece. He was quoted often and widely in the military press, displaying keen mind and caustic wit as well as real concern for the men under him and the innocents it was his duty to defend and protect. Nile Barrabas was on the rise in the System; he was the Army's fair-haired boy.

Their initial crossing of swords was all Heiss's doing. He liked to play games with those he hated. He took upon himself the challenge of undermining the major's good works in Vietnam, of using Barrabas as a dupe to further his own criminal operations. Heiss could not claim credit for destroying the man's Army career, though his actions were directly responsible for the court-martial proceedings brought against Barrabas in 1975.

It was no coincidence that since Barrabas's acquittal and subsequent resignation from the Army, his path and Heiss's continued to intersect. They were both drawn to the same spots on the globe—the trouble spots. Barrabas was a professional soldier for hire and Heiss a peddler in the machinery of death; but neither of them practiced his trade for mercenary reasons alone. Hard-bitten appearances to the contrary, Barrabas was too much of a romantic for that. And, much more than the money, Heiss loved the exercise of power, the big-league risk, the sweet taste of victory.

In defeat, Karl Heiss was always magnanimous. Even though he enjoyed giving the impression he was a good sport, his generosity was entirely pragmatic. In the murky world he inhabited, enemies could become allies overnight. He also thoroughly enjoyed the idea that, win or lose, a heavyweight player such as himself could appreciate a truly worthy adversary. . . like Nile Barrabas.

That was, of course, before Kaluba.

The humiliation of punishment by his "inferiors," righteous punishment, cut through all the pompous bullshit. For months the prospect of revenge against Barrabas, somehow, sometime, was all that held his mind together.

As he sat there on the concrete, eyes glazed, torso rocking rhythmically back and forth, his hands tightened on the grip of the imaginary machete. At first his movements were minute twitches of forearms and wrists; quickly they broadened into wild, overhead slashes. Like an animal, Heiss grunted with each swing, seeing living flesh struck clean off the bone.

He was so absorbed in the mental mayhem that he failed to hear the cell-block door open. Nor did he hear the soft, quick footsteps coming down the corridor. It was not sounds but the lack of them that startled him out of his reverie. The mindless babble, the nonstop racket of his fellow prisoners was cut off as if by a switch, leaving only the steady drone of the generator. He jerked his head around, heart pounding. In the corridor outside his cell were four men with shiny black faces. Coal black except for the white edges of their eyelids and lips. Kentucky minstrels in camouflage fatigues and dark green berets. They carried mini-Uzis, barrel stubs extended by fat, Parkerized tubes...noise suppressors. Frag grenades dangled from their combat harnesses. Two of them had heavy canvas satchels slung over their shoulders.

I am dreaming this, Heiss thought as one of them knelt in front of his cell door and began to pick the lock.

When the door swung open and two men entered Heiss's cell there was a stirring in the air like a faint breeze. It was the whispering of the other prisoners. One of the intruders jammed the beveled tip of a crowbar under the hasp and with a single heave popped it free of the concrete, leaving it and the padlock still attached to Heiss's ankle chains. He could see the rivulets of sweat pouring down the sides of the man's face, the ring of black on his collar where the makeup on his neck had rubbed off.

It was no dream.

It was rescue.

When Heiss was helped from his cell, out into the passageway, all hell broke loose. Realizing that he was about to escape, the other convicts shouted and banged an alarm.

"Shut up, you fuckers!" the lead man in the corridor snarled. He jammed his Uzi's silenced muzzle between the bars of the nearest cage and opened fire, chopping down tightly packed prisoners whose sole defense against 9mm slugs was upraised arms and hands.

The yelling got even louder.

"Come on!" the leader bellowed, running for the exit.

Hobbled by the chains, Heiss could not keep up. Strong hands gripped him under the arms, and for the second time that evening he was dragged the length of the cell block while his incarcerated brothers rained abuse and spittle on him. When they reached the door, the man who seemed to be in command jerked a thumb back at the howling inmates. "Do 'em!" he said.

Canvas satchels were unslung, opened, fuses ignited and high-explosive parcels skidded back down the hallway. As Heiss and his rescuers pushed out the door, the screaming behind them took on a new frenzy.

They were almost all the way to the outer wall when the satchel charges detonated, lighting up the night in a flash of brilliant orange. The earth rocked underfoot and all of them went down hard on the cinders. On his hands and knees, Heiss looked back, squinting against the shower of dust and debris. The cell-block roof had been blown out, the walls broached, and inside their perimeter everything was burning. Then Heiss was jerked back to his feet. Bullets whined overhead, smashing into the wall in front of them. They were taking fire from the guards' barracks.

Two of his rescuers turned, knelt and put up covering fire while the others helped Heiss up onto the top of the wall. For a second he lay there on the edge of freedom, looking around the wall top. Farther down, blue flame flickered, the autofire thunder of an M-60 machine gun rolling, pounding the guards' unprotected flank. Hands reached up to Heiss from the darkness on the far side, and he slid down to them.

Across the dirt road a stake truck waited, its headlights off, engine running. Heiss was shoved into the empty cab. Machine-gun fire stopped abruptly. When it did, there was no more shooting from the prison compound. Heiss heard running feet outside, then the truck lurched as men and equipment piled into the bed. The cab doors opened and blackfaced men jumped in beside him.

"Go! Go!" the man on Heiss's right shouted at the driver as he slammed his door.

They were off in a roar, bouncing down the deeply rutted track.

"Hey, did we nail those fucking assholes, or what!" the driver said gleefully.

"Yeah, we nailed 'em good," the man on the other side of Heiss said.

In the light of the truck's instrument panel Heiss could see only eyes and teeth. The pungent smell of burned cordite was thick in the cab. He turned to the guy on his right, the apparent leader of the strike team, and said, "So, Brookler came through for me, after all."

"Who?" the lead man asked.

"Simon Brookler. He financed this operation, didn't he?"

The lead man laughed. "No way. That old weasel's dead. Got his throat cut in Amsterdam a few months back. They found him floating with the ducks in the Prinsengracht."

Heiss gritted his teeth. So much for his share of the Mogabe diamonds. "Who hired you then?"

"You don't remember me?" the man said. "Maybe it's the blackface." He pulled out a handkerchief and began to wipe the makeup off. Then he turned on a flashlight and held it under his chin. "Well?"

Heiss remembered, all right. "Macatee."

"Yeah, you got it. Macatee from the Nam. It's been a while, huh, Karl."

It had been almost ten years. Macatee was one of the U.S. Army deserters Heiss and ARVN Major General Nguyen Son Ny had hired to police their heroin-smuggling empire. As far as Heiss knew, Macatee still worked for the major general.

"Son Ny did this?"

"Yeah, your ever-lovin' buddy."

Heiss was anything but pleased at the news. "Why did the son of a bitch wait so long to get me out?"

"That's something you'll have to ask him."

For an instant the truck headlights caught a pair of eyes on the road ahead. Red eyes. They vanished into the black wall of jungle that bracketed the lane.

"What's the rest of the plan?"

"We've got a chopper stashed in the boonies not far from here. It'll get us to the coast. There's a ship waiting to ferry us to the mainland. Then we fly to Sri Lanka.''

"What the hell's in Sri Lanka?''

"Son Ny, for one thing. And he's got a present there for you. Something he knows you're gonna like.''

Heiss gave him a pained look.

Macatee grinned. "The present is Nile Barrabas.''

2

The longer Barrabas listened to the heated, almost entirely one-sided conversation the more uncomfortable it made him feel.

The subject was life and death.

And everyone in mortal danger was smiling.

"There's no reason for you or your family to stay here," Erika Dykstra said to the small, red-brown man. "We can move the whole export operation to the Indian mainland and you and Niramala can manage it from there."

T.M. Amirthalingam slid a protective arm around his wife's slender shoulders and with utmost politeness said, "Yes, Miss Erika, I agree wholeheartedly. The only thing to do is to move the corporation off Sri Lanka. But as for my family and myself, we will all stay."

The little woman in the floor-length sari nodded agreement.

More smiles.

Barrabas could see the strain in Erika's face, the frustration building in her eyes. She was convinced that for the Amirthalingams to remain in Colombo was an invitation to disaster.

"If you can't think of your own safety, at least consider your children's," she said, looking pointedly past the couple, at the doorway behind them.

On the other side of the beaded curtain were T.M.'s and Niramala's two teenage daughters. Like their mother, they wore their long black hair pulled straight back and braided into a single thick plait. The curtain, a cascade of rose-tinted glass, tinkled as the girls giggled to each other, their soft brown eyes alight. They were flirting with Barrabas. It was harmless. At fifteen and seventeen, Sheila and Jenny seemed much younger than Americans of the same ages—still children, in fact. On Sri Lanka, courtship and marriage were a long way off for them both. And a shy flirtation with the big, white-haired man was an innocent show of affection.

Sitting on the couch in the apartment were Erika's older brother, Gunther, and T.M.'s only son, Godfrey. Between them was a foot-high stack of adventure comic books. The 260-pound Dutch giant and the bespectacled twelve-year-old were oblivious to the discussion going on around them as they pored over the boy's collection.

Barrabas knew why Gunther was not participating in the argument. Gunther recognized a lost cause when he saw one.

"The danger to us has been greatly exaggerated," T.M. assured Erika. "We will all be fine."

"A Tamil employee of yours was murdered not two blocks from here," Erika protested. "There is a time for honor and a time for honorable retreat."

"We have no proof that Vallu was killed because of his religion or his connection with Netherlands Imports Management," T.M. countered. "It's more likely that his death was the result of an attempted robbery or a random street attack."

"T.M., the only one you're kidding here is yourself. Everything that's happened in the past few weeks—the sudden hassles with the government, the anonymous death threats, Vallu's murder—points to an organized campaign against our company and the Tamils working for us. You wouldn't have called us here from Amsterdam and you wouldn't be suggesting that we move everything if the situation wasn't critical. For God's sake, T.M., you've worked with my family all your life as an equal partner in the corporation, like your father and his father before him. For you to stay on here without Netherlands Imports is senseless."

"Miss Erika, please," Niramala said firmly, "you are forgetting that this is our country, our homeland. We are Sri Lankans first, Tamils second. We will not be driven out. We will not run."

"If the trouble gets worse I am capable of defending my family," T.M. said. With that, he walked over to a nearby closet and took out an ancient pump shotgun and a leather ammunition pouch on a shoulder strap. He showed the weapon to Erika. It was almost as tall as he was. "Believe me," he said, "I know how to use it."

Erika turned to Barrabas, barely able to conceal

her fury, and said, "This is impossible. Nile, do something."

It was not a demand; it was a plea.

Barrabas stared at T.M. The little guy was dressed like a golfer from the late sixties; white-knit, short-sleeved shirt and baggy bell-bottom trousers in a garish orange-and-white plaid. Instead of white golf shoes he wore sandals. Instead of a four iron he held a twelve bore. Barrabas knew exactly what the statuesque blonde wanted him to say. He also knew that it wouldn't work. T.M.'s stand was unconditional, based on emotion rather than logic. No amount of expert opinion on the potential hazards of the situation could change his mind. Until those hazards actually confronted him, T.M. would not be moved.

Beside Barrabas, the aged air conditioner clattered and groaned, sending a weak stream of coolness across his chest. The back of his sleeveless black T-shirt stuck to the vinyl of the dinette chair as he rose. For a foreigner in Sri Lanka, to breathe was to sweat.

"Let me see the ammo," he said to T.M. He looked into the leather bag. The shells were high-base, two and three-quarter inch loaded with Number Two shot. "For waterfowl?"

"Yes," T.M. said. He set the shotgun's butt on the floor in front of his feet, holding the midbarrel between his hands.

"The shells will do, but the gun's no good."

"I'm an excellent shot."

Barrabas moved closer. "It's not you I'm talking

about. The gun's no good. Here, I'll show you why.''
His left hand moved in a blur. He grabbed the thirty-
inch barrel just below the bead sight and shoved it to
the side. As T.M. fought to retain control of the
weapon, Barrabas pretended to draw a handgun
from his belt. "What are you going to do now?" he
said, pressing the tip of his index finger, the muzzle
of a hypothetical pistol, against the man's forehead.

T.M. stopped struggling.

"See?" Barrabas said. "A gun like this is a lia-
bility in close quarters. If you're serious about using
it for defense, we're going to have to do some surgery
on it. Is that all right with you?"

T.M. nodded, handing the gun over.

"This isn't at all what I had in mind, Barrabas,"
Erika said.

He ignored the remark, cracking back the slide
and looking into the open action. The weapon was in
good shape, though all the blueing was worn off the
external metal. He put his finger on the barrel, even
with the cap of the magazine tube. "We've got to
hacksaw it off about here," he said. He tromboned
the slide several times, making sure the gun was
unloaded, then pulled the trigger. There was a dry
snap. He kept the trigger pinned and cycled the action. Every time the slide closed there was another
dry snap. "It's got no disconnector. If you hold the
trigger down, it'll fire as fast as you can pump."

From the couch, Gunther said, "That's real cute,
but I've got a better idea. Why not just go down to
the warehouse and crack open a 'farm machinery'

crate, remove one contraband nineteen-inch Sony Trinitron and take it to the nearest officer of the law? Not only will he trade you his SMG for it, but if you play it cool, you can probably get his sidearm, too.''

The mention of a submachine gun brought young Godfrey out from behind a well-thumbed copy of *Captain Diaz and the Omega Commandos*. But only for a moment.

''No, we can't do that,'' his father said. ''For one thing, there are no more 'farm machinery' crates downstairs. I had the entire shipment of televisions moved to a separate warehouse when customs started taking a more serious interest in the company. If they haven't already figured out where our million-and-a-half dollars worth of black-market merchandise has gone, they'll be sure to follow us right to it. Besides that, I can't afford to be caught with an automatic weapon. It would be just the excuse the government needs for a complete seizure of all Netherlands Imports holdings on Sri Lanka. How long will it take to alter the shotgun?''

''It's not exactly a major undertaking,'' Barrabas told him. ''It'll take all of fifteen minutes.''

''It'll be painless,'' Gunther said.

''I don't believe you two!'' Erika said. ''You're encouraging him in this stupidity.''

''He doesn't need encouragement,'' Gunther said as he returned to his comic book. ''If he's going to stay here, he needs a crash course in urban combat.''

''Have you got a saw, T.M.?'' Barrabas asked.

''Nothing that would cut through a gun barrel, I'm afraid.''

"Then why don't you wrap this up, and then you and I will go out and find ourselves a friendly metal shop."

While T.M. and Niramala set about rolling the shotgun in newspaper and tying the parcel with twine, Erika pulled Barrabas into a corner.

"This is no joke, Nile," she said, looking up into his face. "Colombo is a powder keg. It could blow anytime. Gunther and I can survive if we lose everything we have warehoused here, but I don't want my friends hurt because of their religion. Dammit, I don't want to lose them."

Her blue eyes searched his.

"I know," he said, touching her cheek lightly with the edge of his hand. He had never doubted that her concern was genuine. Or that it was well founded. What he doubted was that there was anything they could do about it. "I'll try and talk to him while we're out."

"You mean it?"

"Mean it. I'm not promising results, though."

"Here it is," T.M. said, presenting the long package to Barrabas. As they headed for the door, T.M. addressed his children. "Girls, I think you still have some household duties to perform this morning. And Godfrey, that goes for you, too."

The boy lowered his comic book and blinked at his father. There was no need for T.M. to repeat the request, however. Heaving a barely audible sigh, Godfrey put down the comic.

As the boy got up from the couch, Gunther patted the stack of magazines. "Don't worry," he said, "I won't eat more than half of them while you're gone."

It was a promise that stopped the boy dead in his tracks. Godfrey's short pants showed off remarkably skinny legs, like mahogany-colored sticks.

"Hey, what's with this guy, T.M.?" Gunther said, reaching out and clamping a great paw around the back of the boy's neck. "He takes everything so seriously."

"If anybody else threatened to eat his library he wouldn't take it seriously," Barrabas said.

"No, T.M., you're just not beating this kid enough," Gunther said.

Godfrey glanced over his shoulder at the huge, seated Dutchman who held him fast. As he did so, he thumbed his glasses back up the narrow bridge of his nose.

The battle of wills only lasted a second.

With a bellow of rage and suitable grimaces, Gunther pretended to throttle the boy. His antics looked ferocious but were so gentle that Godfrey couldn't help but laugh. Gunther let him go.

"That's more like it," he said. "While you're doing your chores I'll go with your dad and the colonel. When I get back we'll read through the lot together. You've got some great stuff there. Real classics. Never thought I'd see the first five numbers of *Cannibal Princess* outside of a museum."

Barrabas and Gunther followed T.M. out the door onto a short landing, then down a steep wooden staircase. The Amirthalingams lived on the third floor of a building owned by the Dykstra family corporation. The second and third floors were given over to clerical and warehouse space respectively. When they stepped out the front door, the heat hit Barrabas like a sledgehammer. Not just the midday sun. The humidity. They hadn't gone twenty steps before his T-shirt was soaked through, front and back.

Gunther nudged him as they walked along. The Dutchman, being in worse physical condition, was even wetter than Barrabas. His fatigue pants were stuck to his thighs, and inside his deck shoes, his socks were sopping. "It's all mental attitude," Gunther said, indicating T.M. with a nod of his head. "Just think cool."

The Tamil who strode purposefully before them showed no effects of the heat or humidity. Apparently the scenery did not bother him, either.

It bothered Barrabas.

According to native legend, Sri Lanka was as close to Eden as one could get in this life. If that was true, then Colombo was a pimple on Eden's behind. And the Pettah, the crumbling district where the Amirthalingams lived, was a pimple perched on a pimple.

The narrow, dusty street they walked was lined on both sides by three-story buildings. Their facades were no more than twenty feet wide, a jumble of different architectures jammed edge to edge, their colors faded aqua, gold, pea green. Litter and garbage were everywhere. As were hurrying people.

Bumper to bumper, cars choked the middle of the street, their horns bleating. Just ahead, Barrabas could see the cause of the tie-up: the right side of the road was further narrowed by a line of parked trucks. Men in loin sarongs struggled, unloading heavy burlap sacks. Like ants they swarmed over trucks and cargo. As Barrabas and Gunther passed, the ants stopped to stare. Hard.

Barrabas stared back. He was more than a head and a half taller than the biggest of them. A white-haired Gulliver. Over the din of the car horns he caught faint snatches of music from a window above. American music. He recognized it at once. The Four Tops were singing "I'll Be There." The sixties rock and roll, the little brown people, the brutal heat, the bedlam of traffic noise: it all stirred memories. Bittersweet memories. Of Saigon. Only it smelled worse here. An intermittent breeze bludgeoned them with the stench of slaughterhouse.

And there was something else different.

The knives.

Most of the men he saw were wearing knives tucked into their waistbands. Not working knives, machetes or Ka-Bars. Kitchen knives. With thin, single-edged blades and no crossguards. Knives for a quick slash and run.

And on every corner they passed there was a street-side sharpening stand, a bare-chested man in a grimy sarong pedaling the wheel. You could not escape the nerve-grating shriek of steel on grindstone.

Barrabas looked into the faces of the people

rushing past him. Men, women, children—there was a similarity about them all. In the tightness of their lips, the expression in their eyes. A psychologist might have measured their panic in pulse rates, dilation of pupils or, more to the point, the number of weapons publicly displayed. Barrabas was no psychologist. He was a professional soldier and his skin was his calibration tool. He could feel their terror hanging heavy in the air like an electric charge.

These people who were afraid were the Sinhalese, Buddhists who made up the vast majority of the island's population. They were afraid of the Eelam Tigers, Tamil-Hindu terrorists from Jaffna in the north, separatists who wanted to divide the island into two states, one Hindu, the other Buddhist. The Sinhalese government-controlled press blamed all the problems of the country—the food shortages, the unemployment, the crushing and widespread poverty—on the terrorists. And it branded all Tamils terrorists.

That the Sinhalese people believed every word was an accurate measure of their gullibility.

Along the street Barrabas traveled, most of the businesses belonged to the minority Tamils. In the country as a whole, more than one-third of industry was run by Tamils. They were for the most part like T.M. Amirthalingam and family: hardworking, honest and devout. And like the Amirthalingams, for their trouble and effort, their success, they were summarily lumped in with the bombers, arsonists and murderers. That assumption was as much due to Sinhalese jealousy as anything else, a jealousy grounded in the form of Buddhism founded and practiced on the island. Unlike other schools of the religion, the Mahayama branch taught that belief alone was enough to carry mankind to salvation. As the Sinhalese were guaranteed redemption in the next life no matter what they did in this one, they did not bother to work at anything. And although they looked with contempt on all who did, that contempt was edged with envy.

T.M. led Barrabas and Gunther under a rusting sheet-metal awning, through a maze of twisted scrap iron and machine parts, into the smoky rear of the metal shop. The proprietor was seated behind a makeshift counter, drinking tea from a cup decorated with black fingerprints. T.M. addressed the man in Sinhalese, then took the parcel from Barrabas and opened it, showing the man what he wanted done. The proprietor nodded uninterestedly and continued to slurp his tea. T.M. spoke to him again at some length, and finally, reluctantly, the man put down his cup. He took the shotgun behind a soot-blackened brick beam, and after a moment the screech of the hacksawing began.

"No problem," T.M. said, smiling.

A problem was exactly what they had. "T.M.," Barrabas said, "we've got to have a talk about the situation here."

The Tamil's expression did not change.

"The way I see it, you're prepared to die rather than leave this place. And you're willing to sacrifice your family as well."

"I am not suicidal. I don't want to die. And my family means everything to me. But I cannot run. Honestly, could you? Would you?"

"I don't have a family," Barrabas said.

"My friend, if you had a family and you ran and they were safe but shamed, what would you have accomplished? Without honor a family is nothing. The Sinhalese are persecuting us unjustly. We have never supported the Eelam Tigers. To give in to a crime would be a crime. My people have been on this island for centuries. It is as much Tamil as it is Sinhalese." He turned to the Dutchman. "Gunther, you can't tell me that you would run if you were in my place."

Gunther did not answer. The grin on his face was frozen, lifeless. Barrabas stared at the blond giant's eyes. They were brimming with tears. Perhaps from the harsh wood smoke that hung like haze in the cluttered shop. Perhaps not.

"What you're telling me," T.M. told Barrabas, "is that this place isn't worth it. Respectfully, that is not for you to say. This place is all we have."

The white-haired man grimaced. It was true. He had no right to judge. After nearly a decade of fighting for pay on foreign soil he had bargained back his U.S. citizenship, but America was no longer his country. He had no country but himself. He put no value on land, on possessions. To a man in his profession, such things were illusions. Whereas T.M. thought in the long term, in generations, family trees, tens of centuries, Barrabas lived in lock time, the fraction of a second between trigger pull and cartridge ignition. As different as they seemed to be, Nile knew that he and the Tamil were much alike. They were both men of honor and duty.

The metalworker returned with the shotgun and its sawed-off barrel. He had cut the thing correctly, but had left a nasty burr on what was the new muzzle.

"Have him file that down," Barrabas said.

It took some convincing to get the man to do the additional work. He saw it as a comment on his craftsmanship, which indeed it was. A look of pure disgust on his face, he carried the two parts away and began filing furiously. When he came back he showed them the two sides of the cut—the new muzzle of the gun and the fifteen-inch length of severed barrel. Unsure which part they meant to keep, he had taken the burrs off both.

T.M. did not comment. He just reached for his wallet.

Barrabas wasn't particularly surprised at the metalworker. He had already seen plenty of evidence of the way the Sinhalese mind worked. The first night in from Amsterdam he had ordered Coke and ice from hotel room service. The bellboy had brought them literally that—bottles of warm Coke and a huge block of ice in a metal pan. It had never occurred to anyone in charge that there was no way to get ice down the slender necks of the bottles. When the ballcock on a hotel toilet broke, a Sinhalese did not repair it, he took his business outside—and expected the paying guests to do the same. And if the fabric of society was unraveling, the Sinhalese did not isolate problems and seek solutions; they razor-honed their steak knives.

T.M. rewrapped the shotgun and barrel in the same package, then led the way out.

Barrabas hung back a second, blocking Gunther's path. "How in hell can you keep smiling over this?" he said.

"Colonel, if I wasn't smiling I'd be crying my goddamn head off. I've known that guy all my life. He's like my brother. His kids are my kids. What's happening here has changed them. It's put up a wall between us. And the bitch of it is, he's right. Under the same conditions, neither of us would run out. You know Erika wouldn't go, either. We'd all stand our ground and make a fight of it."

Barrabas nodded.

"So what are we going to do?"

"A damn good question," Barrabas said, turning for the exit.

Outside, T.M. once again played pathfinder, taking them back via a different route. The panic level in the street had already jumped a couple of notches. Jeeps and troop trucks weaved wildly through the heavy traffic, carrying armed soldiers.

A hundred feet from their destination, T.M. stopped short. Two white police minivans were parked in front of the Dykstra building, and a pair of policemen with Sterling submachine guns stood guard at the entrance.

"Jesus!" Gunther groaned. "Has the shit hit the fan or what?"

T.M. handed Barrabas the wrapped shotgun. "Please, allow me to do all the talking."

When they tried to enter they were stopped and challenged. After T.M. explained who he was, one of the policemen escorted them all up the stairs and through the door of the Amirthalingam flat. The tension that had hovered in the apartment before was nothing compared to what gripped it now.

"So, you decided to come back," said the uniformed man sitting on the couch. He was the only one in the room who was seated. Erika, Niramala and the children were lined up along the opposite wall. On either side of them were four policemen with British .38-caliber Webley-style revolvers drawn. All of the cops had their peaked uniform hats on.

"I thought you'd deserted us," the man on the couch said. He was short, extremely thick in the torso and legs. In a country with a food shortage he hadn't missed many meals. The bulges of fat around his middle and on his back under his arms made his short-sleeved khaki shirt fit skintight in those places. Despite the extra pounds, he looked powerful and quick enough to be dangerous.

"You were mistaken, Sergeant Perara," T.M. said. He introduced his male guests to the policeman.

Perara puffed at a half-smoked cigarette while he sized up Gunther and Barrabas. An ashtray had been placed on the arm of the couch for his use. He tapped his cigarette at it carelessly, spraying ash onto the couch arm and floor. There was a twinkle in his eyes when he spoke. "I've been ordered to bring you and your foreign bosses to customs headquarters to answer some questions."

"This is harassment," T.M. protested. "We have done nothing wrong."

"Under the circumstances," Perara advised him, "I'd keep a civil tongue in my head."

"What circumstances?"

"You haven't heard? Then let me be the first to tell you. The Tamil terrorists are massing for a full-scale assault on the south. It could come at any time. The afternoon papers will be full of it."

"You can say that again," Gunther muttered.

Perara fixed the blond giant with a cold stare. "You and your Dutch friends are suspected of smuggling quantities of arms and ammunition into the country for the Eelam Tigers."

"That's ridiculous!" Erika said.

"We've received a number of anonymous tips about your company's relationship with the terrorists. Those tips must be thoroughly investigated." He stubbed out his cigarette and stood up. "You will come with me."

T.M. started across the room toward his wife and children. He was cut off by policemen and raised pistols.

"Oh, for Christ's sake," Gunther said.

"You will come with me now," Perara repeated.

"It's all right," T.M. told Niramala. "Everything will be all right. They can't possibly hold us. We'll be back soon.''

Barrabas turned with the others and headed toward the door.

"You!" Perara snarled at his back. "Where do you think you're going?"

"Wherever they are," the white-haired man said.

"No. Your presence is not required."

"Stay, Barrabas," T.M. said as he was pushed out onto the landing with Gunther and Erika. "Stay with them."

"Oh, he'll do that," Perara said, grinning obscenely at Niramala and her daughters. "And I'm sure the three of you will keep him well occupied while daddy's away."

Sheila and Jenny moved behind their mother, seeking the dubious protection of her body.

"What I'd give to be in your shoes," Perara said to Barrabas. "Who knows? Maybe someday soon I will." He gave the Amirthalingam women another lewd appraisal. "We can compare notes."

Barrabas had heard enough. He took a quick step toward Perara. Not tight and angry, but fluid, cool. With intent. The move had the desired result. It put a sudden end to the topic under discussion. As Perara retreated behind the line of uniformed men, Barrabas caught himself wondering which way the man's head was threaded on his neck. Clockwise? Counterclockwise? With double-action revolvers pointed at his face, Barrabas knew it was just idle curiosity.

"Be real nice to my friends," he said to Perara. There was no "or else" in his voice; but it was there in his eyes, beneath the heavy, narrowed lids, in the hard, angular planes of his face.

Safe in the midst of his armed lackeys, Perara found the courage to smile. "Don't worry, big man," he said as he backed out the open door, "your turn will come soon enough."

"I'm not worried," Barrabas told him. "I'm counting on it."

3

Karl Heiss smeared three heaping tablespoons of marmalade onto the triangle of buttered toast, then pushed half the slice into his mouth. As he chewed, the bitter orange flavor was so intense it made his jaws ache. When first liberated he had been unable to keep anything substantial down, a result of the starvation rations of maize and beans he had received in prison for so long. After a week of freedom, Heiss felt his appetite come back with a vengeance. Not even the presence of former ARVN Major General Nguyen Son Ny at the outdoor breakfast table could put him off his feed.

"I think it's time we had that discussion you've been so eager for," Son Ny said, his eyes hidden behind the mirrored lenses of his aviator's sunglasses. "Now that you've finally regained your equilibrium."

Heiss looked away from the major general's display of teeth. "Equilibrium." Not strength. Not health. It was a word carefully chosen to stick in his craw. And it did. Ten years had not changed the Vietnamese officer in attitude or appearance. His hair was still coal black, saturated with perfumed dressing and raked straight back. He still sported a nasty little pencil mustache and wore a white silk ascot with his short-sleeved safari shirt.

Beyond the shaded veranda of the plantation house, sunlight reflected blindingly off spikes of knee-high grass. For a hundred yards in all directions the land had been cleared around the mansion. Beyond that perimeter was a thirty-foot-high wall of green: rubber trees and untamed jungle. Just visible at the far edge of the cleared area, straight ahead, a squad of men worked. And much closer in, men in camouflage shorts labored under a pair of red-and-white-striped beach umbrellas. The sun shades were set out even with the rear corners of the house, roughly 150 feet apart. From the men's dress and their raucous good spirits they might have been getting ready for a noontime picnic.

Might have.

Without warning, the morning's serenity was shattered. A long burst of machine-gun fire erupted from under the umbrella on the left, sweeping a section of tree line that arced along one side of the house. The M-60 under the other umbrella answered with a sustained volley of its own to the opposite side. As the echoes of autofire gunshot faded, Heiss could hear splintered tree limbs crashing to earth in the distance. He could also hear shouted curses.

Though the squad working farthest away was well out of the firing lanes, they did not appreciate the unannounced target practice. Understandable, given the fact that they weren't out there picking daisies; they were planting antipersonnel mines.

It was all part of the Son Ny Show.

Heiss reached for the handle of the porcelain coffeepot. Ten years had passed and the major general was still the same. He still adored surprises. Bloody little melodramas of which he was author, director, producer and leading man.

"Go ahead, ask me anything you like," Son Ny said as his guest refilled his cup.

Heiss was hard pressed to decide what he hated most about the man. Son Ny had many irritating mannerisms. He was in the habit of primping in front of every object highly polished enough to give back his reflection. For a man who deceived with appearances and was not deceived by them, this was more strategy than vanity. The peacock was also a vicious, conniving bastard.

"Surely you still have questions?"

Heiss sipped his coffee. Some questions he had already answered for himself. The reason the major general had waited so long to rescue him was easy enough to deduce: Son Ny figured the longer he rotted in prison the more grateful he would be when he was freed. Maybe that was what he hated most about the man. Son Ny so thoroughly enjoyed having Heiss in his debt. The ex-CIA op put down his cup. There was one question he had not been able to answer on his own. "What has all this to do with Barrabas?"

Son Ny made a little A-frame with his fingers, then held it to his chin. "Everything. You will agree that he is a man who has done us both a great deal of harm in the past? He cost us much when he shut down our operation in Vietnam. Alone, that last shipment he intercepted was worth millions. And then he turned you over to the military police at gunpoint. If I hadn't sprung you from the stockade at Tan Son Nhut in '75, you'd still be in an American prison.''

"What about Barrabas?"

"I don't need to remind you that I wanted to have him killed ten years ago, before he could hurt us. It would have been so much simpler then. A sniper's bullet. A helicopter crash. A mine explosion. But you didn't agree.''

"We needed him then," Heiss said.

It was a point that could not be debated. Their drug business inside the U.S. Army camps and for export worldwide had depended on the goodwill of the South Vietnamese National Police Special Branch and the Military Security Service (MSS). Goodwill was expensive. It had required heavy bribes not only in cash and uncut product, but also in heads. Part payment had been made in names of suspected Vietcong legal cadres, agents living overtly in the south with legitimate government ID cards, names painstakingly obtained by Major Nile Barrabas through his "Operation Achilles" program, which dealt with villagers one on one. Barrabas was required to pass these names on to the CIA through Heiss, who saw to it that they went straight to his contact men. Instead of launching a further investigation of people only suspected of being enemy agents, Special Branch and the MSS rounded them up and executed them on the spot, adding numbers to their units' body counts and ensuring that they kept their positions of power.

"We do not need him now," Son Ny said.

"Agreed."

Son Ny smiled. "Sri Lanka is a dangerous place. There are terrorists everywhere. Terrorists who would like nothing better than to disembowel an American. Think how that would disrupt the already crumbling tourist trade! The government and police are fools, incompetents. They can be bought for next to nothing. Believe me, bad things can be arranged to happen here—and at fire-sale prices. Do you by any chance remember Barrabas's girlfriend from the Saigon days?"

"General Hart's daughter?"

"No, the Dutch national."

"Tall, blond, a stunner."

"That's the one. Erika Dykstra. She and her brother own an international import business. It's been in their family for generations. During the war they exported native handicrafts from Phan Rang. The business was a front for smuggling gold, jewels, currency and works of art out of the country. They did some work for the CIA, too. That was a long time ago. The Vietnam setup was only a small part of their operation. One of their main transshipment points is here on Sri Lanka. They have warehouses, offices, employees. I have seen to it that the Dykstras' company and workers have come to some grief with both the government and police. Enough grief to bring brother and sister—and sister's lover—here on the run.''

"Barrabas is in Sri Lanka?''

Son Ny nodded.

Heiss pushed up from the table, his heart thudding in his throat. "What are we waiting for?!''

The major general waved for him to return to his seat. Heiss remained standing. "If it's as easy as you say, let's take a squad and kill him now.''

Son Ny shook his head. "And I thought you'd fully recovered from your little ordeal in Kaluba. I guess appearances can be deceiving where injuries to the mind are concerned.''

"Cut the fucking crap!'' Heiss snarled back. "You think you know how it was in Kaluba. You think you could've held up better than me. You don't know shit about shit. I'm as together now as I've ever been and I'm telling you I want Barrabas's head.''

"Patience,'' Son Ny said evenly, again gesturing for his guest to sit down. "Patience is what is called for.''

The smirk on Son Ny's lips told Heiss that he had lost game, set, match. The louder he protested, the more delighted he would make the major general. Grinding his teeth, he slumped back into the chair.

"If we do not handle this thing correctly,'' Son Ny continued, "we will only stir up a hornet's nest. The white-haired man has friends. Remember the band of mercenaries he employs? The 'Soldiers of Barrabas'?''

Heiss frowned. Could he ever forget? How many of them were there? A dozen, perhaps. And they had singlehandedly butchered and bagged the revolutionary army of Haile Mogabe. True, their success in Kaluba was as much due to the tactical genius of their leader as to their own skill, yet it was clear they were stubborn, determined professionals. "Go on," he said.

"If we do this my way I guarantee you Nile Barrabas will come to us. So will his mercenary SOBs. Sometime in the next forty-eight hours we will be greeting them all."

Heiss looked past Son Ny at the men and the umbrellas. The two machine-gun positions were protected by camouflaged earthworks, connected to each other and the plantation house by a network of sodcovered trenches. There were two more machine-gun outposts at the other end of the house. The four were stationed so that their arcs of fire overlapped, covering the entire perimeter. It was not a defense set up on the spur of the moment. The combined salaries for thirty-five men, the cost of matériel and the bribes amounted to a considerable sum, not to mention the trouble. The price was too high for it all to be just a way for Son Ny to show him up.

"Why all this effort?" he asked. "You wrote off what happened in Vietnam years ago. You don't give a damn about Barrabas. Why all this for me?"

The major general leaned forward. "I want us to

join forces again. This is my way of showing you how much I would value your assistance."

Now it began to make sense. Barrabas was the carrot on the stick. "Join forces in what?"

"I have partners in Paris, other former high-ranking ARVN officers. Together we control a considerable liquid-capital resource. Monies liberated from the treasury of the republic before the fall and other secret funds supplied by American intelligence during the war for their purposes and diverted to ours. We are in the legitimate business of lending capital at a point or two below prevailing interest rates to qualified borrowers. Our only stipulation is that the people who do business with us must take into their employ a few of our men. Vietnamese nationals."

"Vietnamese Mafia."

"Our association operates on a global scale."

"Where do you fit in?"

"My group," Son Ny answered, "handles policy enforcement."

"Kidnap, bombing, assassination...."

"You get the picture. I've kept on a lot of the men who worked for us in Vietnam. The most talented ones."

Heiss had recognized some of the faces. They were guys who had volunteered to fight in Nam because it gave them an opportunity to murder legally. Their talents had been wasted on the U.S. Army, which was too confining for them, too particular about its human targets. And, of course, the pay purely stank. All of them had been deserters when they joined Son Ny and Heiss. A few had been wanted men before they deserted. Macatee, for example. In order to avenge some minor wrong done to one of the string of teenage prostitutes he pimped, he had fragged a downtown Saigon bar, killing ten people to get back at one man. Son Ny may have had his faults, but he knew how to handle men like Macatee, to keep them exercised, top of form and under control.

Heiss did not have to ask how he fitted into the operation. It was obvious. Son Ny's group needed an expert in illegal procurement of automatic weapons, explosives, documents, in transport and logistics—preferably a Caucasian for low visibility. A man willing to kill if the need arose.

"Money is no object in this," Son Ny assured him. "If you'd like, we can discuss terms right now, the how and what of our working arrangement."

It sounded like a sweet deal, all right. Unlimited capital. Freedom of movement. A chance to play the kind of international high-stakes hardball Heiss loved. There was only one problem: the deal would have been even sweeter without the major general. Heiss could already see a definite duplication of function in the enforcement team. He could do Son Ny's job as well as his own. The reverse was not true.

"After you give me Barrabas, we'll talk about our future," he said.

Son Ny's eyes were hidden behind the mirror reflection of brilliant sky and rushing clouds. Under the fine line of mustache his sensual mouth was supremely confident.

"The trap," he said, "only needs a bit of bait. Pretty, pretty bait."

4

Erika stared blankly out the second-story window of the reception room, arms folded across her chest, the fingers of her right hand drumming impatiently on her left elbow. Her face was bathed in golden light. The sun was setting over the Colombo harbor complex. A rusty cargo ship glided past on its way out to sea. Somewhere on the cement quay outside, somewhere close but unseen, a musician was playing a bamboo flute. The tune was wistfully sad and slow. It did not soothe her; in fact, it had the opposite effect. The flutist was playing as if submerged in heavy syrup, sustaining every quavering note. He had all the time in the world.

So did Erika, like it or not.

She glanced over her shoulder at the three dark-skinned men in shirt sleeves talking animatedly on the other side of the office counter. For six hours, she, Gunther and T.M. had been waiting in the Civil Investigation Division's reception room, waiting for someone in authority to make a decision. Their police escort had long since gone.

Gunther sat on the couch with T.M. He was looking at the linoleum floor between his feet, his chin supported in both hands. "What are they doing now?" he asked the Tamil.

"Still arguing over their paperwork protocol."

"Why don't they just ask someone who knows the answer?" Erika said.

T.M. laughed. "Because they're Sinhalese. They'd rather debate the issue round and round. And, in the process, keep us waiting forever. The longer we wait, the more important it makes them. What you're looking at are the remnants of a British colonial bureaucracy perverted by a 2,500-year-old Buddhist caste system. Pure slapstick comedy."

"Yeah," Gunther said without enthusiasm, "so far it's been a laugh a minute."

"For them," Erika said, glaring at the men behind the counter. "They made us sit here and watch while they took two tea breaks and ate their midday meal. What's next?"

"Oh, I think it's a safe bet they'll just disappear," T.M. said.

Gunther looked up from the floor. "Say what?"

"That's right. One by one they'll slip out of the room and take a back exit to the street."

"Without a word?" Erika asked.

"That's standard operating procedure. As far as they're concerned, they've put in a full day's work. I keep forgetting you don't have to deal with this all the time."

"And I keep remembering," Gunther said, "why we have you running things here."

"T.M.," Erika said, "I thought this was supposed to be serious business. Impound. Confiscation."

"It is serious business for us. I knew CID would discover the new location of our contraband sooner or later, but I didn't think they'd work this quickly. They must have had an informant. Now that they've sealed up the warehouse, pending an official inquiry, we stand to lose it all."

"All those Sonys," Gunther said, shaking his head.

"And the funny fellows with the English clothes and the so very British accents over there have the power to take them and everything else. They aren't concerned about the charges against us because they know they aren't true. Netherlands Imports has never supplied arms to terrorists on this island or anyplace else."

"How big a bribe will it take to make them leave us alone?" Gunther asked.

"If we can get off with a bribe it will take a sizable one. It's too soon to put out feelers. For the time being we have to be patient and play it their way. As soon as they sneak off, we can leave. They aren't worried about us jumping the island. In fact, they would prefer it. If we abandoned the holdings of Netherlands Imports, they would get it all without a struggle. Tomorrow, the police will pick us up again and bring us back here. And we will wait some more. It will go on until they get bored with us. Then they'll either deal or try to take everything."

"You have the patience of a saint, T.M.," Erika said.

The Tamil smiled. "No, but to get along here, it does take a sense of humor. The word 'hassle' was invented in Sri Lanka. It's the one area in which the Sinhalese don't discriminate. They do it to their own people, too."

Again Erika glared at the men behind the counter. The idea that they could slink away without even acknowledging her existence was unthinkable. "Will it make things worse if I hassle them back?"

"Worse?" T.M. said. "I don't see how things could get worse."

"That's what I thought," she said, heading for the counter. As she approached, the three men angled themselves so as to present the maximum amount of back to her. "Excuse me," she said.

The clerks paused in their conversation for a moment to look at her in disbelief. The man in the middle dismissed her with a curt wave of his hand, as if brushing aside some lowlife in the street. Then the backs closed ranks and the argument in English resumed.

"Hey!" she said. "I'm talking to you."

This time no one turned around.

Erika grabbed a ball-point pen secured to the counter top by a little metal chain. She snapped the chain with a quick jerk of the wrist. "You!" she said, chucking the ball-point at the back of the middle man's head.

It hit sideways and bounced to the floor.

The man put a hand to the impact site and turned around. They all turned around, astonished.

"Right here, mister," Erika said, pointing at the counter. "Front and center."

As he stepped forward, his associates stepped back. He had a long thin face and a nose to match. "Yes, what is it?" he demanded.

"I want your name."

"B.R. Kotelawala."

"And your immediate superior's name?"

Kotelawala stiffened. "Why do you want to know that?"

"To make a complaint."

Erika looked to the side in time to see the door behind the counter swinging closed. The other two clerks had beaten a hasty retreat.

"I thought you were Dutch," Kotelawala said. "You speak English like an American."

It was intended as an insult as well as a brief diversion. "Thanks," she told him. "Now what about that name? If you don't tell me I can easily find out for myself. How will it look when I tell your boss that you refused to give me his name?"

Kotelawala opened his mouth. No sound came out. The door behind him banged open and one of the men who had slipped out rushed back in, breathless, his eyes wide with excitement.

"They're here!" he said. "The Eelam Tigers! They ambushed an army patrol, killed everyone. The invasion has started. There are already 5,000 terrorists inside the city!"

"What is going on?" Erika said.

Kotelawala pointed angrily at T.M. "Ask the Tamil," he said.

Before she could protest, the two clerks were out

the back door. She turned to her brother and T.M. "Well, Tamil?"

T.M. sadly shook his head.

"GIT AWAY, SHIT FACE," Macatee told the legless beggar. He shifted his shoulders against the brick wall of the alley and returned his attention to the entrance of the CID building across the street.

Almost immediately there came another insistent tug at the exposed tails of his fatigue shirt. Macatee looked down at the filthy, half-naked man. His legs gone clear to the hips, he was strapped to a square scrap of plywood fitted with metal wheels.

"You really want it, don't you?"

The beggar kept on tugging with his left hand and making "feed me" gestures with his right. He rolled eyes brimming with tears of genuine need.

Macatee put his size-thirteen shoe against the edge of the roller board, trapping it against the wall, and knelt down. As he did so, he slipped a hand inside his unbuttoned shirt. At eye level with the beggar he withdrew his hand. Instead of the fat wallet that should have been weighing on his conscience, Macatee hauled out an already cocked Detonics Mark V. He put the muzzle of the compact .45 under the man's chin and pressed up, stretching the man's neck, lifting his face toward heaven.

"You still sure you want it?" he asked, thumbing down the automatic's combat safety.

The beggar attempted to push himself away and,

failing that, did his best to fly, flapping his arms wildly.

"That's what I thought," Macatee said, straightening up. He stepped down hard on the board, tipping it up on its forward pair of wheels, making the beggar cling to the edges to keep his balance. "Now, take a hike. No, wait." He beamed down at the double amputee. "Better make that a roll." Savagely he kicked cart and beggar backward out of the alley mouth into the street. Only the bumper-to-bumper traffic saved the man from further mangling. As it was, he merely rebounded off the rocker panel of a Toyota station wagon and sped away as fast as his arms could propel him.

Macatee wiped the muzzle of the Detonics on his shirttail, then slid it back under his shirt, into the ballistic nylon holster below his left armpit. Every place his shirt touched his skin, the sweat oozed forth. It dripped steadily from under the scratchy support straps of his shoulder holster.

Across the street, a lone taxi waited in front of the CID building. Macatee could see the driver. He had his window rolled all the way down and his head hanging out of it. He looked worried. All the people around him were panicked, shouting, running home to barricade themselves in. The Tigers were coming. Macatee smirked. The taxi driver wasn't waiting at the curb because he had been paid to wait; he was just too scared to move. More scared of the ugly American who had hired him than all the terrorists, real or imagined, on the island. It was understandable. The driver had never looked into the eyes of a terrorist; he had looked into Macatee's.

Two people sprinting down the street collided and armloads of empty glass bottles crashed to the ground. They were heading for the nearest gas station for a fill-up. It was Molotov cocktail time. Oh, yeah, Macatee thought, there was going to be some party tonight.

Behind him there was a resonant thud. Then another. He turned in time to see bricks falling out of the wall on the opposite side of the alley thirty feet away. More thuds. More bricks toppled to the dirt. A dusty man in a loin sarong stepped out of the ragged hole onto the pile of rubble, sledgehammer in hand.

"What the fuck are you doing?" Macatee said.

"It's for when the Tigers attack," the man said. "It's an escape route."

"You are one stupid son of a bitch," Macatee told him, turning back toward the house. His expression brightened at once. A blond woman, a Sri Lankan and a big blond man stepped out of the CID building, walked straight over to the waiting cab and got in. "And you three," Macatee added, "are even dumber."

5

"They should've been back by now," Niramala said. "The government offices are all closed."

"Maybe they got themselves thrown in jail," Barrabas suggested.

"With my husband along, that's not very likely. T.M. knows how to handle himself with bureaucrats and police." Niramala looked up from the stove where she was working. "Girls, have either of you seen your brother?"

Sheila and Jenny were at the sink, washing and peeling vegetables for dinner. Sheila, the older of the two, answered, "He went downstairs a while ago. He didn't say where he was going. Not that he ever does anymore."

Barrabas held back the edge of a curtain and checked the street. It was the tenth time he'd done so in as many minutes. Something was happening. The bedlam of traffic noise had faded away to nothing. And the steady flow of humanity beneath the window had stopped, too. He opened the window and leaned out. Up the deserted street under a darkening sky still shot with streaks of gold he saw the reason for the change. There was a roadblock at the intersection. A military stake truck and a police van had cut off all traffic. Around the vehicles a large crowd of civilians had gathered. Some of the people held burning torches. Some were yelling angrily.

The apartment door opened and Godfrey hurried in. He shut the door behind him, locked it and fastened the safety chain. Then he went straight to the closet and removed the sawed-off shotgun and bag of shells. "Here," he said, handing weapon and ammo to Barrabas.

"Godfrey, what in the world are you doing?" his mother demanded.

The boy pushed his glasses back up the bridge of his nose. "Some government soldiers were ambushed by terrorists today. Now, they're saying the Tigers are in Colombo, hiding in the Tamil homes in this neighborhood, getting ready to attack."

"That's nonsense," Niramala said.

"Army and coast-guard units have sealed off the area for blocks around," the boy went on. "They have Kalashnikov automatics. And there are mobs of Sinhalese behind the barricades, getting drunk. I got close enough to hear them talking. They're waiting for someone from the government or the police to bring them the voter-registration lists."

"The what?" Barrabas said.

Niramala wiped her hands on her apron and came out of the tiny kitchen. It seemed to Barrabas that her face had paled. "The voter-registration lists," she said. "They will tell the rioters which houses and businesses belong to Tamils. They'll know which ones to loot and burn.''

"I'd better have a look," Barrabas said. He quickly thumbed five of the high-brass shells into the pump gun's magazine, tromboned the slide to put a live round in the chamber, then packed a last shell into the magazine.

"I'll come, too," Godfrey said as Barrabas unlocked the door.

Barrabas and Niramala said "No!" at the same instant.

The white-haired man smiled at the boy. "Hey, I'll be right back. I'm not going anywhere without all of you."

Barrabas descended the steep stairs three at a time. He had a feeling in his gut he couldn't shake. A bad feeling. Hemmed in on all sides. And about to be squeezed. When he reached the first-floor landing, the eerie silence outside was broken. Shouts. Screams. Shattering glass. He flattened himself against the entry doorway and looked out. Sweat trickled from his hairline down the sides of his face and the shotgun's checkered pistol grip was suddenly slippery in his hand.

It was Mardi Gras out there.

The Mardi Gras of Hell.

At the far end of the street, people were running wild, smashing windows with rocks and chunks of concrete, breaking down doors, setting fires. Out of the chaos came a macabre kind of order: a middle-aged man burst free of the throng and ran screaming down the middle of the street, toward Barrabas, pursued by a gang of ten Sinhalese youths. They caught up with him twenty yards from the doorway where Barrabas stood, cutting his legs out from under him. He skidded on his belly in the dirt. The ten were on him before he could recover.

Barrabas stepped out of the concealing shadows, the 12-gauge snugged hard against his shoulder. It was a reflex action. He wanted to save the man; his heart told him to fire, but he did not tighten down on the trigger. The chopped-down shotgun was useless past the length of a coffin lid. And he knew if he touched off a warning blast to drive the vultures away, it was sure to bring the government troops down on him. Troops with automatic weapons, communications and containment. His first duty was to protect his friends and get them to safety.

The young men slashed with their kitchen knives and broken bottles while the defenseless Tamil shrieked and tried to roll away. They weren't killing him; they were shredding him alive. Another Sinhalese joined the melee, a Molotov cocktail in his hand. As he lit the gas bomb's rag fuse, he shouted for the others to get back. Then he tossed the bomb, turned and ran. The crash of glass was followed an instant later by the whoosh of igniting fuel. A puddle of orange flame leaped into the black sky. And on the other side of the burning curtain a shadow creature crawled. One step. Two steps. Then lay still.

The dancing pyre light beat against the impassive face of Nile Barrabas. As he looked straight into the stinking pit, the depths to which only humanity can sink, he felt a familiar cold at his core. It was not bred of dispassion or disinterest, but of lessons learned painfully long ago. Lessons, even now, painfully applied.

More rioters were pouring around the troop truck at the intersection, ignoring the already trashed stores, moving down the street to get fresh pickings. It was time to clear out.

Barrabas raced back up the stairs. When he entered the apartment he found the Amirthalingams at the windows. They had all seen what had happened below. The three women were horror-struck, but the face Godfrey turned toward Barrabas was expressionless, his dark eyes empty of reaction, of revulsion or fear.

"That's how Vallu screamed," the boy said in a daze.

"Get back from the windows!" Barrabas ordered them.

As Niramala turned away, the window exploded inward and a fist-sized chunk of concrete bounded onto the floor. From the street outside there were angry shouts.

"We can't stay here," Barrabas said. "And we can't use the street. Can we get to the roof?"

"Yes," Niramala said, "from the landing outside the apartment door."

"Grab what you need and let's go."

Godfrey had anticipated the evacuation. He had his entire comic-book collection neatly tied into two bundles.

As Barrabas led them out of the apartment, sounds drifted up the stairwell from the floors below. Laughter, curses and the thud of crowbars on crates. The mob was already in the ground-level warehouse helping themselves. Then came the sound of bare feet running up the stairs.

As Niramala opened the door that led to the roof, the owners of the running feet appeared on the stairway below: three wild-eyed, breathless young men in loin sarongs. Two of them waved meat cleavers. In one hand the third held a quart whiskey bottle filled with gasoline and plugged with rag and in the other a disposable lighter.

Barrabas leveled the shotgun at them. This was the range the weapon could cover. Again, Barrabas didn't want to shoot for fear of attracting a more powerful enemy.

The Sinhalese youths sensed his dilemma.

"Throw it! He won't shoot!" one of the knife-wielders shouted. "Throw it! Burn them up!"

In the heat of the moment, the shotgun was no deterrent. Barrabas might as well have been pointing a broomstick at them. The crazy with the bomb lit its fuse and threw, aiming it at the Tamil family.

Inexperience or excitement or just plain stupidity made the toss high and weak. Barrabas stepped into the path of the lobbed bomb and with one hand snatched it out of the air.

The grins on the faces of the Sinhalese youths turned suddenly sick.

"Go!" Barrabas yelled at the Amirthalingams.

As they ran up the short flight of stairs to the roof, their would-be murderers bolted in the opposite direction. He gave the Sinhalese a count of two heartbeats, timing his throw so the Molotov cocktail crashed against the wall of the stairwell above their heads just as they reached the landing. Gasoline rained down on them, then with a horrible air-sucking rush the landing exploded in flame. Burning, screaming tumbleweeds rolled around the corner and down the stairs, out of sight.

Barrabas turned from the pall of smoke and tongues of fire licking up the wallpaper and hurried to the roof. The family waited for him, huddled together. Sheila and Jenny were crying in each other's arms. Godfrey stood beside his mother, his hands firmly grasping the string ties that held his library together. From the street below came desperate, dying animal sounds. More Tamils had been caught by the mob.

"Is there anyplace in Colombo that's going to be safe for you?" Barrabas asked Niramala.

"The Hindu temple. They wouldn't attack a sacred place. Other Tamils will be hiding there, too." She pointed across the jumble of rooftops, some tiled and sloping, others flat like the one they were on. "It's that way."

Barrabas trotted to the rear edge of the roof and looked down. In the narrow alley below an ant line of looters scurried, bearing their spoils on top of their heads. "The nearest Sinhalese building," he said to Niramala. "Which way?"

She pointed the same direction as before. "Five buildings over is the first."

Barrabas counted rooftops and swore under his breath. The middle building was on fire, smoke boiling out of the lower stories. He climbed over the ledge and onto the tiled spine of the adjoining roof. The drop was only four feet, but the tiles were old and loose. He set the shotgun on the ledge and helped Niramala down. Then Sheila.

As he reached out for Jenny, the night was ripped by gunfire. Full-auto gunfire. Then the flat whump of rifle grenades. Valiant Sinhalese troops were helping the mob break into a well-defended storehouse across the street.

"Come on," he said to the girl.

Jenny could not move. She trembled visibly, paralyzed with fear.

Barrabas looked at Godfrey and started to speak. There was no need.

Two precious bundles hit the roof simultaneously. Godfrey hurried to his sister's side, gently pushed her to the edge and into Barrabas's arms. Then the boy climbed down with the others. He did not look back at the comics he had left behind. They were just dead weight.

It was grow-up time. Grow up now or maybe never.

Barrabas recovered the shotgun and shepherded the family across the back side of the roof, up onto the top of the next building. It was nice and flat, easy going. When they got to the far edge of its roof and

stared down at the middle building, smoke was beginning to seep between its roof tiles, and the heat
could be felt like a solid wall. Barrabas handed
Godfrey the shotgun and jumped onto the roof. He
put a hand to the tile and quickly jerked it back.
Too damn hot. The Amirthalingams were not
dressed for a fire walk. And the smoke was getting
thicker by the second.

"I'll carry you over," he told Niramala. The
Tamil woman climbed into his arms. She was so
light that it startled him. She was terrified, too,
though she did not want to show it in front of her
children. She clung to his neck with desperate
strength as he quick-footed it across the roof spine.
He set her down on the ledge of the next building,
then went back for the others. He carried Godfrey
last. Godfrey carried the shotgun. The boy did not
close his eyes or bury his face in Barrabas's chest as
his sisters had done. He watched in detached fasci-
nation as firelight flickered between the gaps in the
tile directly below.

Barrabas deposited him alongside his sisters and
took back the 12-gauge. He was touched by the
boy's bravery. Touched and concerned. The white-
haired mercenary had seen kids even younger than
Godfrey, hardcases, doing a man's job and doing it
well. War, revolution, terror were the magic po-
tions that either put maturity on one's bones or left
them stripped, bleaching in the sun. That did not
make it right. Nothing could make it right.

On the roof of the Sinhalese building, Barrabas

paused at the door leading down. "Once we're inside, and when we get out into the alley," he told the family, "you've got to do exactly what I tell you. No questions. No hesitation." He looked into Jenny's tear-reddened eyes. "Just do it."

The girl nodded that she understood and tried to smile.

The short, darkened stairway ended at a door. Barrabas opened it and stepped out into a dimly lit hallway lined on both sides by scarred wooden doors. An apartment building. No, tenement was a better word. The corridor was so narrow that Barrabas could almost touch both walls with his extended arms. And it was full of smells. The stink of burning real estate outside mingled with the smell of chilis scorching in someone's kitchen. Of garbage. Of a plugged-up loo. The smells of habitation. Dense habitation.

"Come on," he said softly, leading the Tamils toward the end of the hall and stairs heading down. They descended one flight without incident. As Barrabas started them down a second, he heard voices and footsteps coming up the stairway.

"Back!" he said, waving the family up the stairs again. He ushered them into the hallway above and made them stop a third of the way along, their backs to the wall.

As he stood there, waiting, hoping that whoever it was would continue up the stairs to the next story, he realized he was making a puddle on the floor. Sweat. It was like coming out of a shower with all his clothes on.

The sounds got louder and louder and then two men turned the corner of the landing and walked straight down the hall into Barrabas. They stopped jabbering, walking, breathing. Their arms were loaded down with looted goods, cheap radios, toilet paper, bottles of booze. They stared into the muzzle of the sawed-off and the sawed-off stared right back, like the open end of a piece of sewer pipe.

"No noise," he warned.

Whether it was the sight of the gun or the huge, smoke-blackened man wielding it, the looters panicked, dropping their prizes, turning, running, yelling one word at the top of their lungs.

"Tigers!"

Barrabas did not shoot. He and the Amirthalingams had other more pressing problems. Doors all around them were opening. And the narrow hallway was suddenly full of flashing knives.

"I'VE HEARD OF ALTERNATIVE ROUTES BEFORE, but this is ridiculous," Gunther said to the back of the cab driver's head.

"The roadblocks, I'm going around the roadblocks."

Gunther scowled at the view out the taxi window. The driver was running back alleys like a rat in a maze. Traffic was nonexistent, but the general direction seemed wrong. The Dutchman nudged his sister, who sat to his right in the middle of the rear seat. "What do you think?" he asked.

"I think he's lost," Erika said.

"Hey, T.M., is this jerk lost or what?"

Before the Tamil could answer, the cabbie swung the car hard to the right, then roared down an alleyway just wide enough to take it.

"What the hell?" Gunther demanded. Through the windshield he could see a dead end ahead.

The driver slammed on his brakes, hurling Gunther, Erika and T.M. against the back of the front seat. In the glare of the headlights, men poured out of a doorway on the right. Out the back window, in the taillight's infernal glow, Gunther saw more men running up from behind. White men. All of them. And all of them armed. Some with guns, some with lengths of pipe.

The cab driver opened his door, trying to get out. The door only swung four inches before it met the opposing wall. A man standing in front of the right fender raised the automatic pistol in his hand. Then, at almost the same instant, there was a thundercrack report, the windshield spiderwebbed, and the driver's brains and blood splattered the side of Gunther's face.

"Oh, Jesus," he groaned. "Jesus!"

The car shuddered as a pair of men jumped on the back bumper, then rocked. With a crash the rear window's safety glass went suddenly opaque. Gunther threw his body across his sister's a second before the window yielded to iron pipe, showering them with bits of glass.

This is it, Gunther thought. This is fucking it.

There was another gunshot.

One Gunther did not hear.

One hundred fifteen grains of jacketed hollow-point beat the thunder to his skull.

6

There were no questions asked in the dim corridor.

No IDs requested.

No time-outs.

Jenny shrieked in pain as a savage downward stab pierced the back of her arm. She stumbled away, falling to her knees, clutching at her wound.

"Down!" Barrabas snarled, pivoting with the stubby, quick 12-gauge hard against his hip. As the Tamil family flattened, he fired, aiming at the hand and knife poised to strike Jenny in the back. The muzzle belched a yard of flame, the hallway reeled under the earsplitting boom, and the knife vanished.

The hand remained. Sort of. A mangled nightmare jetting blood.

Barrabas did not pause. Shotgun trigger pinned, he pumped back the slide, swinging the barrel in a tight, controlled arc. The high-brass hull was barely airborne when he snapped the action closed. Again the terrible boom, the brilliant muzzle-flash. A straight-on chest hit stopped the charging, knife-waving man as if he'd run into a solid wall. He crashed to the floor on his back, legs pistoning, taking him nowhere.

Niramala screamed from behind and Barrabas spun, tromboning the slide. Again the boom, this time partially muffled. The man running at his back got close, really close. Shot in the gut from a range of less than twelve inches, the man was blown off his feet, slammed against the wall; his polyester shirt melted away from a cavernous hole. He flopped to his face, a ragman.

"More?" Barrabas shouted at the stunned on-lookers, chucking the smoking hull to the floor. "You want more?"

They wanted none. Doors slammed shut, locks clacked and the hallway was again empty, except for the newly dead.

Barrabas helped Jenny to her feet and quickly examined the slash wound. It was painful but shallow, no tendons severed, and she wasn't losing much blood. "You're all right," he said to her. "Can you walk?"

She nodded, but her eyes said something different. She was drifting into shock. Barrabas picked her up. "Hang on to my neck," he said, shifting her negligible weight to his left arm. "Now, everybody hit the stairs. On the double!"

At the door to the alley, Barrabas stopped, moving Jenny slightly to free the fingers of his left hand. He then turned the shotgun belly up and fed it three live rounds. "Stay close together," he warned the Amirthalingams.

As they pushed out the door and merged with the flow of drunks and looters someone in an upper story of the building leaned out a window and screamed, "Murderers! Stop the terrorist murderers!"

No one in the alley paid any attention. The Tamil family looked no different from their Sinhalese neighbors; they were invisible. And the rioters were much too intent on maintaining a firm grip on toasters and tape cassettes, too keenly interested in what the person next to them might drop.

Barrabas was the only one to draw stares. For one thing, he was carrying another human being instead of some bright, inanimate object, and a pretty, slender girl at that; for another, his appearance was startling. It was not just his physical size. Even though his white hair was darkened by soot, it was still a stark contrast to the black grime mixed with body oils and sweat that coated his skin. Beads of fresh perspiration cut tiger stripes down the sides of his face and along the powerful muscles of upper arms and shoulders bared by his sleeveless T-shirt. Those who stared at Nile Barrabas did not stare long.

He and the Amirthalingams were swept along by the current of greed to alley's end. There an army six-by-six was parked, its open tailgate partially blocking the exit. Soldiers with Sterling submachine guns and Kalashnikovs were looting the looters, taking what they wanted and loading it into the truck.

Barrabas lowered the sawed-off, holding it along his thigh. In the press of people trying to get out with what they had, the soldiers' hurry to confiscate the largest and most valuable merchandise, the gun went unnoticed.

At Niramala's instructions they turned left at the alley mouth and again at the first street. From several blocks over came the sounds of more government intervention: automatic gunfire and grenade blasts. The pattern was clear to Barrabas: any place the mob met resistance was classified a "terrorist stronghold" and troops were called in to provide necessary additional firepower.

He did not have to ask what part of town they were approaching. His nose told him. The abattoirs. They hurried down a narrow lane, flanked on both sides by windowless plaster walls, tile and tin roofs and open gutters. The street was deserted; there was nothing to steal except rats. Rats the size of Lhasa apsos were feeding on slaughterhouse liquid waste in the gutter trough. As Barrabas and the family came close, the creatures broke ranks and fled, staggering, weaving as if drunk. One of them never made it out of the gutter. It fell onto its side, twitching violently in the throes of death. Poisoned.

"How much farther?" Barrabas asked Niramala.

"Around the corner," she answered.

The lane doglegged to the right, then opened onto a much wider avenue. Straight across the intersection was the temple. It was four stories high, its steeply pitched tile roof crowded with shadowy, twice-human-sized statues of Hindu deities. The doorway to the temple was also twice man size, and people were straggling through it from both directions.

Gunfire erupted again. This time much closer than before.

As Barrabas and the Amirthalingams dashed across the intersection, heavy trucks swung around the bend to their right, engines roaring. Pinned in the headlight beams were other madly running Tamils. Tamils with no chance of survival. From the cabs, running boards and beds of trucks, soldiers shot wildly, their ricochets whining angrily overhead. All the doors along the street were locked except the temple's, and they were rapidly closing.

Barrabas shouldered the doors back and pushed T.M.'s family through the gap. As he put Jenny down, he looked up the street. The headlights of the lead truck bounced as its front wheel hit a thing in the road. A thing that had been a person.

He slipped into the relative cool of the temple and helped a trio of Tamil men shut and bolt the doors. Solid iron plate, inches thick, hinged on the inside, the doors were indeed pieces of work. They would absorb a lot of punishment.

Barrabas turned and surveyed the torchlit interior. Clustered around a rectangular fountain pool were many Tamils. People of all ages, some nursing injuries, sat on the low, mosaic tile wall, praying, weeping. They believed as Niramala did that the Sinhalese wouldn't dare attack a sacred place. On the other side of the heavy doors were screams, single shots and the squeal of brakes. Barrabas was not so sure they had reached refuge.

He found the Amirthalingams. Niramala was dressing Jenny's wound with a makeshift bandage. The girl seemed to have recovered a bit. Sheila tore a strip of cloth from her sari, dipped it in the pool, then stepped up on the wall. On tiptoes she began to wash Barrabas's face. He did not pull back. The water and her touch felt good.

"You saved us," Sheila told him, wiping down his arms. She gazed up at him with brown eyes full of adoration.

"Come out!" an amplified voice bellowed from the street. "Throw out your weapons and come out. You will not be hurt."

"I haven't saved you yet," Barrabas said grimly. "Godfrey, come on. I need a quick tour of this place and a view of the street."

The boy led him up a stone staircase to the darkened second floor. Spaced along the wall facing the street were windows covered with heavy ornamental metal grates. Hard yellow light streamed through them.

Barrabas squinted against the glare. Outside, the army trucks were lined up with headlights pointed at the temple entrance.

"Surrender your guns, come out and you won't be hurt," repeated the bullhorn voice.

Barrabas scowled. Only an idiot, a blind idiot, would have believed the promise. Visible in the trucks' lights, the corpses of those shot in the back, crushed under the wheels of the six-by-sixes, lay sprawled in the middle of the road.

"I know that voice," Godfrey said. "It's Sergeant Perara."

The speaker paced agitatedly in front of the high beams. "This is your last warning," he shouted into the bullhorn.

It was Perara, all right. And he wasn't hiding. He knew exactly whom he was up against. Not armed terrorists, but unarmed merchants and their families. More meat for the grinder.

An army officer consulted with Perara briefly, then dispatched a squad of uniformed regulars up the street.

"What's that way?" Barrabas asked the boy, pointing in the direction the soldiers had gone.

"Around the corner is the entrance to the temple garden."

"Show me fast."

Godfrey ran ahead, taking him along a corridor open on the inside to the fountain and people below. What Barrabas saw down there was too damned many people for one man to defend. They passed through an arched doorway and out onto a rear balcony. In the center of the garden was a shadowy spirelike structure as tall as the temple. From it, gravel paths radiated through the trees and flower beds.

"The gate is over there," Godfrey said, pointing to the left.

"Is there another way in or out?"

"There's a small gate in the back wall. You can't see it from here. It's too dark."

Barrabas handed the boy the shotgun and slipped a leg over the balcony railing. "Drop the gun to me after I climb down. Then go tell the people to keep well away from the front doors." He indicated the arched balcony door with a nod of his head. "Make sure you shut and lock that one after you."

Using the decorative stonework for hand and footholds, he quickly gained the ground. "Drop it," he said softly.

The 12-gauge fell neatly into his hands.

Avoiding the gravel, sticking to the deep shadow next to the building, Barrabas turned and ran, tight-roping the tiled back border of a long flower bed. Close. He had to get close. The heavy crunch of feet dropping to gravel from a height made him stop short. The soldiers had already scaled the garden's gate. He jumped down and took cover behind a statue. The soldiers talked in hushed tones as they advanced down the path toward him. Cocksure. And why not? They had been sent to rout lambs from a temple. It was an operation they knew they could handle.

Barrabas dropped to all fours and peered around the base of the statue. He ducked back at once. Six of them, all in a nice tight bunch. Stay that way, he thought. Stay confident. Stay dumb.

When the footfalls were almost on top of him, he bit the tip of his tongue. The pain obliterated his fatigue, gave his mind, his anger, a diamond-hard focus. He vaulted from concealment to the middle of the path, shotgun waist high.

The soldiers were not ready for him. Not ready for a figure so big, so near. Not ready for a weapon so utterly devastating.

The sawed-off boomed and bucked as Barrabas pinned the trigger. Pinned and pumped, jamming 12-gauge detonations end to end. The soldiers' bodies jerked back in time to the staccato blasts, their unfired weapons flying.

As strong as he was, Barrabas could not control the stubby muzzle. At the nearly full-auto rate of fire, there was no time to recover from recoil. The shock of each successive shot drove the point of aim higher and higher until the last shot was a clean miss. His final intended target did not return fire but turned tail.

After what he had seen the soldiers do on the street outside, Barrabas would take no prisoners.

He knocked the man face down on the gravel, then straddled him, driving the shotgun's butt into the back of his head, over and over again. The weapon's steel butt plate did nothing to soften the horrendous blows. Only when the thrashing beneath him stopped did Barrabas let up.

He quickly retrieved two of the dropped AKMs. They had 30-round magazines and wooden furniture. As he searched for a third, there was an explosion. The ground jarred underfoot, and the temple behind him shuddered. Grenades were hammering at the front doors. Weapons cradled in his arms, Barrabas raced for the rear entrance. Godfrey was waiting there and let him in. Another volley of grenades smashed at the doors, shaking the ancient building from foundation to roof, filling the air with clouds of choking dust and screams. Barrabas ran through the midst of the terrified refugees and stepped up on the fountain ledge.

"The back way out is clear now," he shouted at them. "There is a gate and you can all get away to safety. If you stay here you'll be trapped and murdered. Go now and I'll hold the soldiers off as long as I can. Go!"

As the people started hurrying out, he turned to Niramala.

She anticipated his question. "We have a friend in the Muslim part of town. Ahmad Hussein. We will be safe there." She gave him the address. Then she and Sheila helped Jenny up and got her moving for the exit. Godfrey remained behind.

"I want to stay here with you and fight," the boy said. "I'm not afraid."

"You can't," Barrabas said. "Someone has to protect your mother and sisters." He gave the boy the shotgun and ammunition pouch. "Use it only as a last resort. Keep your target within six feet. Understand?"

Godfrey nodded.

"Go on, beat it. I'll catch up later."

"I'll always remember you," the boy said solemnly. Then he ducked out the back door.

"Kid," Barrabas said to thin air, "you read too many comic books."

A trio of dull clunks resounded off the temple doors. Metal on metal. Then an explosion in ragged triplicate that brought not only dust but also bits of rubble down from the ceiling. The hand grenades had been thrown prematurely, bouncing off their intended target, blowing up in the street. Sooner or later the soldiers would get the timing right and the doors would come down. Barrabas had to do his damage before that. He shouldered the AKMs and sprinted up the stairs.

He peered out one of the grated windows. The mob had caught up with the army. They were behind the line of trucks, yelling encouragement to the grenadiers, throwing rocks and the occasional Molotov cocktail. It had not occurred to them that a stone temple wouldn't burn.

Barrabas picked up one of the Kalashnikovs, charged the operating handle and thumbed the fire-selector lever to the middle, full-auto position. He eased the pillar front sight through a hole in the grate. The weapon was equipped with night sights, but he didn't need them. All his targets were neatly illuminated by truck headlights. There would be no problem with muzzle climb, either. Thanks to the grate, there was nowhere for the muzzle to go.

He snugged the rifle butt to his shoulder and took a deep breath. As he exhaled, he tightened down on the trigger. The AKM began to chug, spitting a bright stream of Commie brass from its ejection port, spitting a hot stream of Commie lead from its snout. Barrabas stitched a line from one end of the truck barricade to the other, slicing through the milling soldiers and looters at chest height, splintering headlights, windshields, puncturing radiators and tires. Everyone hit the dirt. Some for the last time.

When the AKM came up empty, Barrabas abandoned it, letting it hang by its trapped front sight, and threw himself to the floor, face against the wall. The window grate exploded inward as a rifle grenade hit it dead center. Bits of hot metal sang around the hall. When things quieted down he rolled over. The acrid smoke was billowing away, moving deeper into the temple. Then a searchlight cut through the smoke and dust, sending a shaft of light through the window opening.

For the first time Barrabas saw that the corridor was decorated with huge mosaics of the Hindu gods. Gazing down on him with perpetual delight was Sri Kali, the goddess of destruction, her belt dangling freshly severed human heads like some obscene charm bracelet. The white-haired man knew the bitch well. All over the world he had seen her handiwork. She was chaos, the end of all things, the inevitable. Not a warrior's ally but his most hated enemy. Sri Kali never took sides. She could not be controlled or courted. Only madmen willingly served her; yet every creature who drew breath was in her employ. She was not something to rail against, to fight; she was something to be accepted.

The rules of the game were forever beyond negotiation.

Barrabas pulled the remaining, fully loaded

AKM from the rubble and bellycrawled to the next window grate. Again he put the weapon on full auto, fitted the front sight through an ornamental opening and pressed the trigger.

With a crash, the searchlight winked out. Barrabas dropped his point of aim. He saturated the left front fender of the middle truck with 7.62x39mm lead, dumping the rest of the mag into the area where he knew the gas tank was strapped. Before the last round was spent, he was rewarded. A brilliant orange flash consumed the front half of the vehicle, and the explosion tossed flaming rain on other trucks and the people hiding around them.

Barrabas dived away from the window and buried his head under his arms. A salvo of rifle grenades blew out the grate, whistled into the temple interior and detonated on the floor below. Small-arms fire raged from outside, pouring through the window opening.

Having done all he could, Barrabas was ready to make a discreet and timely exit, but the sound of an engine revving made him pause. It was a big engine and in need of a tune-up. It kept backfiring. He put his back to the wall and straightened up, angling himself so he could sneak a peek without putting his head in the middle of fifty pairs of sights.

Across the intersection, at the mouth of the lane that he and the Amirthalingams had traveled, there was an ancient bus. The driver was tromping on the gas pedal, sending plumes of whitish smoke aloft. Even as Barrabas looked on, there was a screech of protesting gears, then the bus lurched forward between the parked trucks, motor howling. It was going to ram the temple doors.

Barrabas bolted for the corridor and the balcony beyond. He had one leg over the railing when the motorized battering ram struck. The resounding crash and scream of ripping metal shook the whole structure.

It was definitely time to go.

7

Barrabas was relieved to find Niramala, Sheila, Jenny and Godfrey all safe at the home of their Muslim friends, the Husseins. However, his relief was short-lived.

"We've had some bad news," Niramala said straight away. "It's about Erika, Gunther and T.M."

"Not dead," he said.

"No, nothing like that. T.M. contacted us from a hospital nearby. He said there had been an accident and that you should come at once."

"What are we waiting for?"

Niramala shook her head. "T.M. doesn't want us to go there. He forbids it."

Barrabas did not like the way that sounded but said nothing about it. "Give me the directions."

She also gave him the ward and bed number.

What with the riots there were no cabs on the streets, so he had to walk. The night was full of sirens, distant gunfire and wood smoke. The Muslim section of Colombo was untouched by violence for the time being. Also a minority in Sri Lanka, they were as hated by the Sinhalese as the Tamilis for the same reasons: diligence, thrift, hard work. The Sinhalese preferred to keep the minorities separate, as history had taught that the two combined were capable of seizing and holding power by force.

When Barrabas set foot in the hospital foyer, he knew why T.M. had forbidden his family to come. The place was a horror show, packed to overflowing with victims of the riots. The burned, the raped, the mutilated lay on gurneys in the halls, sat shivering on the floor awaiting treatment. The smell of roasted human flesh was as overpowering as the bedlam of moans, cries and shrieks for help.

He worked his way through the ocean of pain and suffering, dreading what he would find when he reached his friends.

"Barrabas! Wait!" someone shouted.

It was T.M. He was in one piece, walking, no bandages.

"You're all right?" Barrabas asked.

"Yes, of course," the Tamil said. "Gunther is over there in bed."

The white-haired man hurried to the bedside.

"You did good, Nile," Gunther said. "You got T.M.'s family to a safe place."

Barrabas looked at the bandage that covered half of the Dutchman's head. "What did you walk into? A chunk of concrete?"

"I think it was a 9mm."

"Cop gun?"

"You'd better sit down," T.M. told him.

1. How do you rate _____ ?
   (Please print book TITLE)
   - 1.6 ☐ excellent   .4 ☐ good   .2 ☐ not so good
   - .5 ☐ very good   .3 ☐ fair   .1 ☐ poor

2. How likely are you to purchase another book in this series?
   - 2.1 ☐ definitely would purchase   .3 ☐ probably would not purchase
   - .2 ☐ probably would purchase   .4 ☐ definitely would not purchase

3. How do you compare this book with similar books you usually read?   X1
   - 3.1 ☐ far better than others   .4 ☐ not as good
   - .2 ☐ better than others   .5 ☐ definitely not as good
   - .3 ☐ about the same

4. Have you any additional comments about this book?
   _____ (4)
   _____ (6)

5. How did you *first* become aware of this book?
   - 8. ☐ read other books in series   11. ☐ friend's recommendation
   - 9. ☐ in-store display   12. ☐ ad inside other books
   - 10. ☐ TV, radio or magazine ad   13. ☐ other _____
   (please specify)

6. What *most* prompted you to buy this book?
   - 14. ☐ read other books in series   17. ☐ title   20. ☐ story outline on back
   - 15. ☐ friend's recommendation   18. ☐ author   21. ☐ read a few pages
   - 16. ☐ picture on cover   19. ☐ advertising   22. ☐ other _____
   (please specify)

7. Have you purchased any books from any of these series or by these authors in the past 12 months? Approximately how many?

	No. Purchased		No. Purchased
☐ Mack Bolan	(23) _____	☐ Clive Cussler	(49) _____
☐ Able Team	(25) _____	☐ Len Deighton	(51) _____
☐ Phoenix Force	(27) _____	☐ Ken Follet	(53) _____
☐ SOBs	(29) _____	☐ Colin Forbes	(55) _____
☐ Dagger	(31) _____	☐ Frederick Forsyth	(57) _____
☐ The Destroyer	(33) _____	☐ Adam Hall	(59) _____
☐ Death Merchant	(35) _____	☐ Jack Higgins	(61) _____
☐ The Mercenary	(37) _____	☐ Gregory MacDonald	(63) _____
☐ Casca	(39) _____	☐ John D. MacDonald	(65) _____
☐ Nick Carter	(41) _____	☐ Robert Ludlum	(67) _____
☐ The Survivalist	(43) _____	☐ Alistair MacLean	(69) _____
☐ Duncan Kyle	(45) _____	☐ John Gardner	(71) _____
☐ Stephen King	(47) _____	☐ Helen McInnes	(72) _____

8. On which date was this book purchased? (75) _____

9. Please indicate your age group and sex.
   - 77.1 ☐ Male   78.1 ☐ under 15   .3 ☐ 25-34   .5 ☐ 50-64
   - .2 ☐ Female   .2 ☐ 15-24   .4 ☐ 35-49   .6 ☐ 65 or older

Thank you for completing and returning this questionnaire.

NAME _____

ADDRESS _____

(Please Print)

CITY _____

ZIP CODE _____

NO POSTAGE
STAMP
NECESSARY
IF MAILED
IN THE
UNITED STATES

BUSINESS REPLY MAIL

FIRST CLASS   **PERMIT NO. 70**   **TEMPE, AZ.**

POSTAGE WILL BE PAID BY ADDRESSEE

NATIONAL READER SURVEYS

2504 West Southern Avenue

Tempe, AZ   85282

"Where's Erika?"

"Like T.M. said," Gunther repeated, "you'd better sit down for this."

"Let's hear it."

"We got jumped after we left CID," Gunther said. "Not by rioters. These guys were white, well trained and well armed. They killed the cab driver, shot me and took Erika."

"It was all my fault," T.M. said. "I shouldn't have let them take her. I should have fought them. I should have done something."

"Don't be dumb," Gunther said. "There was nothing anybody could do."

Barrabas knew that was the truth. If all 260 pounds of Gunther couldn't protect his sister, she couldn't be protected. "So what do these guys want? A ransom?"

"Yeah, but not money. They want you," Gunther told him. "And you're gonna shit when you hear the rest of it."

"I was told by the kidnappers to give you a message," T.M. said. "From a Mr. Son Ny and a Mr. Heiss."

Barrabas's eyes narrowed.

"They say if you want Erika back alive to come and get her. They told me where she is being held. A rubber plantation near Matale in the central highlands."

"This is for real?" Barrabas asked Gunther.

"I think I recognized a couple of the men who attacked us. They used to work for Son Ny in the Nam days."

"Then Heiss is out of Kaluba, too?"

"Yeah. Most likely. What do you think about this plantation bit? Do you think she's really there?"

"Sounds like Son Ny, all right. Daring me to walk into a trap."

"Should we go to the police?" Gunther asked.

"No, thanks," Barrabas said. "I've seen how the police work here. I'm going to try and call in the squad. They could stand an island vacation. And this island could stand a dose of them."

Gunther winced as if in sudden pain.

"Say, are you really okay?"

Gunther put on a happy face. "Yeah, it was just a crease. They had to shave a patch the length of my head. Can't wait to get a look at the new hairdo. Figure I might start my own international fad."

"Yeah, wash, blow dry and flesh wound. Gunther, you are weird."

"I'm gonna get even weirder if you don't get my sister back," he said.

"You and me both. Hang in, I'm going to go make that phone call."

T.M. followed him out of Gunther's earshot, then said, "I have one more thing to tell you. I didn't want to say it in front of Gunther. Those men told me there is a time limit. If you don't successfully free her in forty-eight hours, they will execute her anyway."

"Thanks for not telling him," Barrabas said. "He's in no shape to go busting through the bush, and we both know that's exactly what he'd do."

"I want to help you in any way I can. Not just because it's Erika they've got. I owe you. What you did for my wife and children is something I'll never be able to repay."

"When I get off the phone I'll need to make some arrangements. You can help me with that. In the meantime, why don't you go see your family. I know they're worried. And you can't do anything more for Gunther tonight. Go on and I'll meet you over there later."

The nearest operational phone was in Barrabas's hotel. The walk over and the time he spent waiting in line to use it gave him a chance to think things through. The main problem was that the mercenary team he led wasn't set up to function the way it had to in this situation. Barrabas was an independent contractor working covertly for the U.S. government. The government came to him through a supposedly nonaligned intermediary, another independent, Walker Jessup. A man known in Washington's rarified circles as the Fixer. The portly Texan only had the power to offer Barrabas work and discuss monetary terms. The former U.S. Army colonel could accept or reject either out of hand. There was a necessary distance between Jessup and the Soldiers of Barrabas. He knew who they were and what they had done because he had helped put the team together, but he never had any direct contact with them. His bosses on Capitol Hill wanted to minimize all traceable links between themselves and the mercenaries doing their dirtiest of dirty jobs.

In this case, contact between the SOBs and Jessup was unavoidable. Stuck on Sri Lanka, with a time deadline hanging over his head, Barrabas had no other way to locate, pull together the men and requisite matériel and arrange transport for all of it. He knew Jessup could handle the job, but he had qualms about the man personally. He made it a habit never to trust anyone who had ever taken money from American intelligence. Sneaky petes had screwed up his life too many times in the past. Like that slimeball Heiss. Even though they were on the house payroll, they always played for themselves. Barrabas had worked with Jessup on and off since Vietnam, and the fat man had never crossed him up. That didn't mean he wouldn't if the need or opportunity ever arose.

As he stepped into the phone booth, Barrabas put all the distracting concerns from his mind. Erika was in grave danger. What had to be done would be done.

And God help Walker Jessup if he picked this one to louse up.

8

Walker Jessup hung up the phone. His ear was sore, his neck stiff. He pushed his bulk from the oversize executive swivel chair and stretched. Since Barrabas's urgent call two hours earlier, he had been talking nonstop to his own private network of operatives and to old buddies high up in the U.S. intelligence community, trying to get things rolling.

It wasn't easy.

Favors asked meant favors granted in return. That was the way the business was run. Give and take. A form of barter Nile Barrabas refused to deal in. He was one hell of a combat tactician but in no way a horse trader. Jessup, on the other hand, could put a saddle on steak tartare and collect a stud fee.

The favors he needed on this hurry-up mission were many and large. He had to have immediate secure transportation and entry-exit documents for paramilitary personnel. Read: Agency transportation and documents. Jessup was up to the minute on the situation in Sri Lanka. It was what the embassy in Colombo called "fluid." Read: Proceed at your own risk. Accordingly, he had to get complete immunity for all those involved in case someone in a government uniform stepped into a bullet.

What surprised even an old ex-CIA hand like Jessup was the response from his pals at Disneyland when he mentioned the possibility of Karl Heiss's being involved. His name was the magic key that opened all the doors. The CIA had been hunting Heiss for almost ten years without success. Rumors of his death, though frequent and widespread, always proved to be greatly exaggerated. Karl Heiss had the habit of slipping the noose just as the trap-door dropped away.

Barrabas had been after him for as long as the CIA had. Several times over the years, the white-haired man had come close. In Casablanca in 1979 a mutilated corpse was found with obviously forged ID bearing the photograph of Karl Heiss. The body turned out to be a plant left behind to throw off the narrowing pursuit. If Barrabas had only chosen to kill his old enemy after their last encounter on Kaluba instead of dropping him into the hands of the local penal system, the current hassle could have been avoided.

Jessup knew it was easy to second-guess. And from what he had heard about the island nation's medieval concept of justice, it was exactly what Heiss deserved.

He lumbered over to his office wall safe and twisted the dial through the unlocking sequence. From the steel vault he removed a flat leather case. He released the catch and the lid sprang back. Inside, on textured foam padding, was a custom Colt Combat Commander with black neoprene wraparound grips and three loaded stainless-steel magazines. Jessup thumbed out one of the .45-caliber cartridges. The hollowpoint slugs were specially made with extrawide, extradeep nose cups. Nose cups that would each hold a marble.

It had been a long time since Jessup had fired a shot in anger, although he put in his four hours a week at the practice range. The idea of going out in the field again was something he had not even considered. He couldn't move the way he used to. And a man of his size encountered unique difficulties in a world designed for more compact physiques. Such as airline seats that perfectly fitted one of his buns but not two. And bathroom doors he could not squeeze through with a full bladder. Not to mention the fact that food in the Third World was notoriously unpredictable.

The idea of being forced to diet because of some nasty indigenous microorganism made him feel suddenly famished. He put down the bullet and the gun case and turned to the office sideboard where an untouched club sandwich and triple-thick chocolate shake awaited him.

Some men were made for a life of action. No matter what they put in their mouths they never gained a pound. Even in his youth, Jessup had been cursed with the metabolism of a tree sloth, but when he turned thirty, things went from sloth to slug. He had made a decision back then, a decision he knew he could live with for the rest of his life. No more field work. Stay in D.C. and pull strings.

He picked up a quarter of the club sandwich, four inches of choice cold cuts neatly speared together by a red-cellophane-tassled toothpick. He could see the bacon in there—crisp, salty.

"Shit!" he said, dropping the sandwich back to the plate.

He couldn't look at it in the old way anymore. Not now that his butt was on the line. Instead of a taste delight, it was just another eight ounces of blubber to haul around. Under fire.

It was part of the good old give-and-take. He had to go along on this job and personally do the number or the CIA wouldn't agree to help. He picked up the pistol and practiced a few one-handed magazine changes. It was just the kind of deal Barrabas would never understand. He hoped to hell the big guy never had reason to find out about it.

Jessup's office intercom buzzed. "Yes, what is it?" he said into the box.

"Your tickets to JFK and SFO just arrived, sir," a disembodied female voice answered.

"Call me a cab."

Jessup packed the Combat Colt back in its case, then slipped the case into an official diplomatic pouch. He locked the pouch and pulled on his tent-like suit jacket. Then he chained the pouch to his right wrist.

As he worked, a highly irritating thought kept preying on his mind: Manhattan was blessed with some of the finest restaurants in the world, and in good conscience he wasn't going to be able to partake of so much as a fucking after-dinner mint.

Jessup made a meaty fist.

If O'Toole gave him any crap, any crap at all. . . .

EVERY TIME the red-haired man so much as laid a finger on the leggy brunette, she screamed. Not bloody murder. Not rape. A piercing shriek of passion.

Why isn't this fun, the red-haired man asked himself. Why do I feel like a credit dentist from Jersey? He playfully tapped the nude woman on the shoulder and was rewarded with yet another squeal. Maybe I'm just not sloshed enough to enjoy it, he reasoned. With that, he rose rockily from the apartment couch. Once he gained his full height he blinked twice, then plummeted back to the cushions as if his bare butt was cast in concrete. He was drunk enough. Better than most men alive, Liam O'Toole understood the fine line between stupor and coma.

"Do you want to hear my sex fantasies?" the brunette asked coquettishly.

Two hours earlier that had been O'Toole's fantasy as he had sat in the Greenwich Village bar, listening to the unpublished poetess read from the crumpled pile of loose-leaf paper that was her collected works. Her poetry was on subjects as diverse as her interests: romantic love, death, *la condition humaine*. And all of it stank. When she started reciting an ode to her cat, Fatso, the similarly un-published poet-patrons of the bar pelted her with wadded-up moistened cocktail napkins and booed her off the tiny platform stage.

Whiskey in hand, the gallant O'Toole had crossed the room to console her. "I'm a battlefield poet," he had told her.

"How nice for you," she had replied.

As they had exchanged winning smiles, he had sneaked a quick upsidedown peek at her work and verified what he had already suspected: she put circles instead of dots over all her *i*'s. No, it wasn't her writing style that had attracted him. Under her carefully ironed denim workshirt were a pair of the most perfect metaphors he had ever seen.

"I'd really like to share my fantasies with you," the poetess went on earnestly.

O'Toole put his hand on her knee.

And she nearly went through the roof.

This lady brought a new dimension to the word "sensitive." Her reaction was so loud and so violent that he instinctively jerked his hand back.

She batted her eyelashes at him, then said, "I've always wanted to be. . . enslaved."

O'Toole had a brief vision of nude brunette poetress trussed up like the holiday bird and sudden-ly coma didn't sound so bad.

"My whips are all at the dry cleaners," he said, lurching to his feet.

"You have a belt, don't you?"

"No, darlin', that's what I need." He dumped the

last of the fifth of Bushmill's into a water glass, raised it and said, "Scotty, beam me up."

Before he could get the glass to his lips, the apartment doorbell rang. He carried the whiskey to the door. When he opened it he looked up at a huge overweight man with a case manacled to his wrist. "What do you want?"

"O'Toole, you're naked," the fat man drawled.

The Irishman looked down at himself and nodded. "So?"

"You're also shit-faced."

"Two out of two."

The fat man glanced over O'Toole's shoulder at the woman on the couch.

"No, don't," O'Toole said, waving his hand. "Let me guess. She's naked, too?"

"We've got serious business to talk. Get rid of her."

"I don't know you and if you don't move your foot, you're gonna lose it."

"My name's Jessup and it's about the colonel. He's in big trouble."

"Anybody could say that. I still don't know you."

"Chen, Boone, Biondi," Jessup said. "They all have one thing in common. They're still in Iran."

O'Toole grimaced. His three mercenary comrades would be in Iran forever. Part of the air, the water, the dirt. Nobody outside the SOBs knew that. "Who the fuck are you?"

"Dump the girl."

"Yeah." O'Toole put the whiskey down on a lamp table and confronted the brunette. Having overheard the conversation at the door, she had already started to pull her clothes on. "Sorry to cut the evening short," he said through an enormous grin. "Maybe we can do it again? That is, if you're not already tied up."

"I don't think you're a poet at all," she said. "You couldn't be. You're too insensitive."

"Hold it!" O'Toole shouted as she made for the door.

The poetress stopped in front of the fat man.

"Touch her skin," O'Toole told him. "Go on, touch her anywhere on bare skin."

Jessup shrugged and put a finger on her neck.

Nothing.

The brunette pushed his hand away and stormed out of the apartment.

"What the hell was that for?" Jessup asked.

"A test. Either you got it or you don't." He removed his boxer shorts from the lampshade and pulled them on. Then he padded into the bathroom and stepped into the shower stall, shorts and all.

As he turned on the water and adjusted its temperature, the glass shower door opened a crack. "What're you doin' in here?" O'Toole asked the fat guy.

"Making sure you don't drown."

"Just make sure you don't try to get in here with me. That doorway's mighty narrow and I don't want to lose my security deposit on this place."

"You got nothing to worry about," Jessup said, reaching in and shutting off the hot water.

O'Toole didn't even flinch.

Jessup explained the situation as O'Toole soaked his head under the frigid spray. By the time he finished hearing it all, he had sobered up considerably.

"How're we going to locate the rest of the SOBs in San Francisco?" Jessup asked him. "I've got no addresses for them."

O'Toole reached for a towel. "Those guys have been out on the coast for three days. By now, they're all staying at the same address."

"City jail?"

"Smart fella."

9

"This is your last, I repeat, your last warning," said the amplified baritone. "Come out or we're coming in to get you."

Nate Beck bent the venetian blinds down with a fingertip and peered out the window. The North Beach side street below was choked with police cars, their lights flashing. The SWAT team van was in position along the opposite curb, parked in front of a strip club called Birds of Paradise. Above the van's roof, on the club marquee, a pair of electric nipples blinked. A neon come-on.

"Hey, Nate, trust me," said a voice behind him, "it's really not a trip to San Francisco without a visit from the Tac Squad."

Beck let the blinds snap back. Billy Two, the six-foot-six-inch half-Navaho, half-Osage, was straddling a chair backward, grinning his head off. Emilio Lopez, perched on the edge of a wobbly dressing table, was likewise much amused.

"You got to learn to relax more," the Mexican American told him. "Take life as it comes."

Beck couldn't help but worry. It was in his nature. In his goddamn genes. And there was real cause for him to have the jumps. The small matter of a computer theft of a million bucks. A "perfect" crime that no one would have ever known about if his wife hadn't blown the whistle on him. Nate Beck was a wanted man on two continents. And SWAT was about to kick in the door.

"This," the wiry Lopez said, making an expansive gesture with his arms, "is a once-in-a-lifetime experience."

Beck glanced over at the trio of females lined up with their backs to him and knew in his heart that Lopez was right. The sheer alabaster majesty of all those naked bottoms was awe inspiring. He also knew that if he had any sense at all, he'd walk over to the little redhead, the one who'd been so impressed when she'd found out that he was a professional soldier of fortune, and take the golden opportunity to get to know her better. But no. There they were, barricaded in the second-floor dressing room of a topless-bottomless club with the entire road cast of *Campus Nude-in* and all he could think about was consequences.

"In case you hadn't noticed," Lopez went on in a more confidential tone, "not only are our lady companions marvelously muscled, highly trained artistes, but two of them are definitely natural blonds."

"I noticed," Beck said. "And maybe I would've had a chance to do more than notice, if you hadn't broken the bouncer's arm."

"Hey! The guy grabbed my new shirt. I told him

not to mess up my threads." The shirt in question had been bought at an antique clothing store on their first day in town. So far as Beck knew, Lopez hadn't had it off since. It was part of a bowling team uniform for the Ace Condom Company of Kansas City, Missouri, circa 1950. Embroidered over the breast pocket was the name Pookie. "And besides," Lopez added, "the pinhead *cabrón* came at me with that frigging stick."

The stick lay on the floor of the dressing room where the bouncer had dropped it. It was actually an old table leg, bored out and filled with a lead plug. Captain of any debating team.

Lopez was not through. "If someone's gonna take the heat for our current predicament, I think we all know who that someone should be." He glanced meaningfully over his shoulder at Alex "The Greek" Nanos.

The bronzed body builder had one of the nude dancers cornered and was talking with her in hushed tones, using a lot of hand gestures. He was big on hand gestures. And blondes under the age of twenty-three.

"The guy's in love," Billy Two said.

As if that explained anything.

Beck was not satisfied. After all, it was his butt in the blender. "Nanos knew up front that the girl danced in the buff. Christ, he dragged us here three nights in a row to catch her act! Now, after their personal relationship has, shall we say, warmed, all of a sudden he doesn't want her to display her stuff to the paying customers, the Jaycees from the tour bus. Now, he won't even let her out of the stinking dressing room because she wants to dance. And the other girls won't go on without her."

"Dancin' is their life," Lopez said.

"And we're all going to jail."

"Hey, Nate, it's not a trip to San Francisco without a visit to. . . ." Billy Two let his words trail off.

Nate Beck winced. The Tac Squad was coming, their steel-reinforced SWAT boots thudding up the stairs.

"You'll thank us tomorrow," Lopez told him.

BECK HAD THE SINGULAR MISFORTUNE of being put in a holding cell with the love-struck Greek. All Nanos wanted to talk about was his new girlfriend, Sunny. All Beck wanted to talk about was why they hadn't been fingerprinted and booked yet. A procedure guaranteed to bring him to the attention of the federal heat.

"Be honest with me now, Nate," Nanos said. "Isn't she the most fantastic-looking woman you've ever seen?"

It occurred to Beck that they had had this conversation before. As recently as ten minutes before. "She's won-der-ful," Nate answered. It was no lie. Sunny was unique. She had a body without flaws. Perfect from every conceivable angle, every distance. Too perfect overall to suit Beck's tastes, though her flanks made him want to bang on the table with his fists and shout macho inanities. He was heavily into flanks.

"And what about her mind, huh?"

Beck was tempted to make a joke, but decided against it. The cell they were confined to was only six by six; there was no place to run. "She's got a great body," he said diplomatically, then tried to change the subject. "I know this isn't SOP for the San Francisco Police Department. It couldn't be. They should have strip-searched me, fingerprinted and photographed us by now. What in hell are they waiting for?"

"Is it so wrong of me to ask her to retire from the stage?"

"Wrong? What could be wrong? You've known the girl three whole days."

"Holy shit, that's what I keep telling her. She says her folks taught her to be proud of her body. Dancing naked is like a statement, a beautiful positive statement she makes to the world."

"Oh, God," Beck groaned softly, sagging back against the cell's metal-sheathed wall.

"What am I gonna do? When I think of her up there on the stage, expressing her philosophy of life, and these slimebuckets off the street sitting there, drooling into their two-drink minimums, it makes me crazy." Nanos paused, regained his composure, then said, "Tell me the truth, what do you really think of her?"

Beck shut his eyes. He couldn't stand to look into that forlorn *pagliaccio* face anymore. It was an object lesson administered against his will: the bigger-they are, the harder they fall. Alex Nanos was a man's man—tough, fearless, skilled with all manner of weapons. He was also a woman's man—a professional woman's man. A grand master with the short stick. A candidate for the Gigolo Hall of Fame. But given the right combination of pulchritude, moon phase and electrochemical imbalance, no man is immune to stupid cupid.

Then a uniformed officer walked up and opened the cell door. "Out," he said. "Both of you."

Beck could envision the whole sequence of events that was to follow. The booking, the discovery of his false ID, the detailed fingerprint check. When the FBI compared the print records of Stallone, Randolf, and Beck, Nathaniel, the "Aha!" would be audible for miles.

"How's the food in Leavenworth?" Beck asked the officer as they joined him in the hall. "Do they give you fresh vegetables?"

"I don't know what you're talking about," the officer said, leading them out of the lockup area. "You wild-asses know some people who can really yank the strings. We were asked to detain you, that's all. No charges have been filed. No nothing. You were never here. And you're free to go."

"Strings?" Beck said as they stepped into the waiting room.

"Yeah, you got those two to thank." He pointed at a stocky red-haired man in a Windbreaker and a mountain in a three-piece suit.

"It's O'Toole," Beck said.

"Yeah, good old O'Toole," Nanos said. "But who's that with him? Shamu?"

10

Erika Dykstra sat like a mannequin, her hands tied behind her and through the back of the massive mahogany chair. If evil could have a smell, a distinct odor all its own, it was there in the room with her. It was the sickly sweet stink of Son Ny's hair dressing.

"You know he will come for you," the major general said, leaning closer to her. "But whether he comes or not, your fate will be the same."

Erika could see her own face reflected in the mirrored sunglasses, its features stretched, distorted by the curvature of the lenses. It looked very pale.

"Do you have any idea what twenty-five healthy, virile men can do to one woman if given the opportunity?" he asked.

"It was explained to me in detail on the way up here," she said flatly.

"Of course I will be the first," the major general said.

Erika wondered if there were really eyes on the other side of the mirrors. Or only raw sockets, packed with squirming maggots.

"I am a skilled lover," he went on, his peppermint-scented breath gusting against her face.

"As a student in Paris during my youth I fre-
quented all the brothels. I learned many ways to
please a woman. I know I will please you. It will be
a wonderful memory to cling to while you are en-
during the attentions of my mercenaries."

Son Ny turned to Heiss, who stood off to the side,
looking out the window. "And what about you,
Karl, will you ride second?" The major general
chuckled as if he'd made a fine joke.

The idea of being forced to take a hairless rodent
like Son Ny between her legs made Erika's skin
crawl. The idea of being attacked by Heiss as well
made bitter bile rise in the back of her throat.

"Oh, look. I think I've startled her," Son Ny
said. "Not to worry, pretty lady, that is the one in-
dignity you will not have to suffer. Mr. Heiss does
not care for the pleasures of the flesh."

"Shut up," Heiss told him. It was a hollow command. Without force.

"My business partner is a monk," the major
general continued with relish. "His joys are all
cerebral. He is a product of cool Teutonic loins, a
mating in the dead of winter. What sort of erotic
dreams do you think such a creature has? You do
have erotic dreams, don't you, Karl? Do you wake
up afterward, heart pounding, and find gold coins
between your belly and the sheets?"

"Shut up!"

Son Ny shrugged. "No sense of humor, either.
On the whole, quite a dull fellow, wouldn't you
say?"

Erika said nothing. It was the only safe thing to do under the circumstances. She didn't want to anger either of them.

"Barrabas has no chance," the major general said, as if reading her mind. "No chance whatsoever of getting you out. Though for the game to have any spice, it must seem to him that he does. You see, I enjoy nothing more than an unfolding of inevitability, a process of gradual, helpless realization. I've arranged it so your lover will have little trouble penetrating the boundaries of the plantation and an impossible time leaving. As soon as you were brought in, my troops activated the perimeter defenses I've had installed. We are an island in the middle of an island, surrounded by mines, booby traps and wonderfully imaginative ambush positions. It is what I believe is called a 'Chinese finger trap,' a children's toy. So easy to stick your fingers in, but when you try to pull them out...."

Erika looked away from the display of teeth. Nile Barrabas was a military genius. When he was under pressure, his mind was like a computer, categorizing, analyzing, evaluating every conceivable scenario. But even more than that, Barrabas had the fighting instinct. He could sense which way an opponent was going to move. And he had the strength of will to wager everything on that unshakable feeling in his gut.

She remembered too well the stories about the major general from the Vietnam days. His involvement in the drug trade had been an open secret and it had been rumored that his private hit team of American deserters were even worse than the VC when it came to making examples of people who got in the way of business. She knew also what Heiss and Son Ny had done to Barrabas, how they had destroyed Operation Achilles in order to maintain their protected status within the corrupt republic. Barrabas cared about success and failure only in human terms and that was exactly how they had hurt him. He had gotten the peasants, the uncommitted fence sitters, to trust him, to believe in him, to put their lives in his hands. Lives that were traded away by Heiss and Son Ny like so many heads of cabbage. Whenever the man with the white hair looked back on Vietnam, the disaster he saw was personal; the pain he felt could only be numbed by booze, booze and more booze.

A pair of faces appeared outside the window opposite her. Grinning faces. Two of Son Ny's mercs were leering at her, anticipating the fun to come.

Erika glared back, her pale blue eyes full of defiance and hate. Then she found a reason to smile.

Son Ny had never fought Nile Barrabas face-to-face before. The major general had always hidden behind "the system," behind the innocent. He had a surprise coming. Erika knew Barrabas as well as anyone could ever know him. She knew that by now the program was already punched in, that no matter what happened to her the readout would be the same.

These animals were dead.

11

Barrabas downshifted and twisted the throttle of the BSA 750 wide open. The power surge of the "borrowed" motorcycle nearly put his behind on the back wheel. He veered the bike around a daisy chain of buffalo carts traveling down the middle of the narrow road. Over the redlined BSA's whine, he could hear the steady jingle of cart bells ringing at every plodding step of beast, every lazy sway of cart.

Once past the obstruction, he slipped the bike into a higher gear and really roared, whipping under the arch of jungle foliage, vines, trees, tropical flowers that overhung the road. The tarmac stretched out before him was alternately washed with brilliant sunlight and plunged in deep shadow. In a patch of light, by the side of the road, a group of women dried rice on woven mats. They were a blur and then they were gone.

He slowed to take a sharp turn and was treated to a spectacular view of forested ridge. He slowed even more and looked back over his shoulder. A mile down the rugged canyon he could see steeply terraced hills, orchards and paddy fields; all were so green it hurt his eyes to look.

It hurt his heart, too.

The Sinhalese youth who had unwillingly donated his motorcycle to Barrabas's cause had shouted at him, "*Pe su menia!* You are crazy!"

Maybe so.

He cranked the accelerator and surged away, rear tire spinning, chucking pebbles off into space. He left behind a blue cloud of exhaust. What he felt inside he could never leave behind. It was as much a part of him as the color of his hair. Hair once dark chestnut brown. That was before the VC river ambush, before a fragment of 57mm shell and his head had made sudden, violent contact. If the shard of red-hot metal had been an inch to the right, his helmet wouldn't have opened up like a can of Spam; if it had gone an inch to the left, he'd have been dead. Either way, his hair would never have turned white from the shock of a near fatal head wound. It was not the most terrible scar he carried, only the most visible.

There were worse things than almost dying.

Much worse things.

That's what Vietnam had taught him.

Sri Lanka was teaching him something different. That for him Vietnam wasn't over. Not just the powerful rushes of memory, the flashbacks triggered by a snatch of sweet sad song or a green-terraced vista. The evil. That would never be over as long as Heiss and Son Ny lived. They had been the enemy then as much as the Vietcong. They were still the enemy.

On top of the mountain, Barrabas wound through a series of S-turns, then braked as he came upon a recently abandoned coconut-rope-manufacturing operation. He shut off the bike. The humid air dripped with the smell of rotting coconut. Coconut hulls bobbed in a slime-covered softening pool. In less than twenty-four hours, if things went right, T.M. would lead the SOBs to this garden spot. It was the final staging area for the attack and rescue.

He hid the motorcycle in the bush, popped a handful of salt tabs, shouldered his canteens and knapsack and moved deeper into the dense jungle. He carried no weapons but his hands and feet. And his mind. There was no way he could've brought an assault rifle through all the army roadblocks between Colombo and Matale. Besides, there was to be no contact, if possible. He would penetrate, sketch the plantation's defenses, return to the assembly area and await rendezvous.

Once safely out of view of the road, he stopped, unslung the pack and took out a cake of camouflage makeup, which he applied to his face, neck and arms. Also from the pack he took a pair of heavy fabric gloves, which would give him some measure of protection from the unfriendly flora and fauna of the Sri Lankan highlands.

For some the tropical jungle was a foreboding place. The canopy of trees and vines formed a smothering blanket in the already oppressive heat. For Barrabas it was like going home. With the thin veneer of civilization peeled back, everything was so simple, so clear cut. Life and death were served up steaming on the same plate.

He consulted his compass, oriented himself to the paved road, then moved slowly on. He had to take his time. Not only was his own life on the line, but if he overlooked anything, it could cost the lives of everyone involved, including Erika's.

His objective, the rubber plantation, was a good two miles away, connected to the main Matale-Kandy road and the coconut rope mill by a dirt track that twisted through the bush, over hilltops and through small summit valleys.

T.M. had provided him with a government topographic map. An X marked the spot where the Tamil believed the plantation house to be. The primitive jungle road leading to it was not on the chart. If the topo map couldn't give him the particulars of human improvements on the terrain, it could give him a good idea of the general features. Ridge lines. Gullies. Possible water obstacles. According to the map, the plantation sat atop an eroded peak, a flat table of land with gradually sloping sides that merged with the much more steeply rolling country below and surrounding it. T.M. had drawn a circle around the entire area to represent the rubber-tree groves planted there.

The ridge lines leading up to the high ground were the best and easiest avenues of approach. Barrabas knew there would be fewer trees and less underbrush to contend with, and animal trails to follow. He also knew the ridges would be closely monitored and defended, certainly by mines and booby traps, possibly by troops.

The most difficult way up would be through the valleys. That would mean crossing streams, gullies, fighting through the heaviest vegetation. The valley route also meant going down before going up— more exertion before the terrible physical drain of combat. Barrabas was already putting his mercenaries on the spot. According to the book, a soldier needed a minimum of seven days to acclimate to the heat and humidity before entering a jungle war zone. The SOBs would have less than one. Professionals fought better when they were mad. Without a valley trek there was going to be plenty of mad to go around.

And then there was the dirt track. It was the easiest to defend with mines and ambushes. The road was also the quickest way out if things went sour for Heiss and Son Ny. Would they risk mining their only fast exit? Barrabas thought they would; but they would be very selective about it and only bracket an ambush kill zone they had already picked out. The dirt road was probably the most dangerous of the three routes to take because it would be protected by the most personnel, but it had to be checked out first.

Barrabas moved off parallel to the dirt road, through the jungle. Visibility was no more than ten feet and the going was maddeningly slow. After an hour and a half by his watch, he stopped to take some water and some more salt tabs. He estimated that he had covered no more than a quarter of a mile. While the dirt road to his right ran relatively flat and straight, the course he was taking rose and fell with the surface contours. It occurred to him that he wasn't the only one with problems. Son Ny had more than a few of his own. He had the high ground, but he also had an enormous area to defend. The solution was obvious: don't defend all of it. Most of his force would be concentrated around the plantation. The other defenses would be unmanned, unselective: mines, booby traps and the like. It was also obvious that the ambush positions would have to be close in, as well. Close enough for a quick retreat to the plantation if there was a hitch or the ambushers met successful resistance. The fixed site or sites would be manned round the clock until contact was made.

Barrabas screwed the lid back on his canteen. If he could locate the primary ambush position and find the covered and concealed withdrawal route, he and the SOBs had their way in.

He moved cautiously to the edge of the road, held aside a broad green banana leaf, and looked both ways. The "road" was actually two tire ruts with a mohawk fringe of grass sticking up between them. Fronds, tree limbs, more banana leaves arched over it.

Something at his feet caught his eye.

The sensor wire should have been covered. Barrabas knelt down and exposed a two-foot length of it. He gave Son Ny's men the benefit of the doubt.

Maybe the wire had been covered. Maybe rain had washed the dirt off.

He knew there had to be ground sensors there, because they were the most practical way of monitoring traffic on a two-mile length of road when manpower was limited and a canopy of jungle cut down the range of radio transmission.

Barrabas backtracked along the road until he found the end of the line. The first sensor in the string. The spot had to be permanently marked for future reference. He moved another hundred feet up the roadside, then found himself three football-sized rocks. He set them on the road in a straight line, working them into the soft dirt so they would not be dislodged by a passing vehicle, so it almost looked as if they belonged there.

He stared down the deserted track. Either side of it could conceal an ambusher. The foliage formed a dense curtain impossible to see through. But there was a big difference between concealment and cover. Barrabas stepped back into the bush and resumed his patient, careful advance.

By four in the afternoon, the strain had begun to get to him. By his estimate he was within a quarter of a mile of the plantation and he still hadn't found what he was looking for. He was beginning to think that he hadn't given Son Ny enough credit. That maybe the major general had some trick card he hadn't anticipated. Then something jumped in the trees ahead. A monkey or a bird. Barrabas told himself he would have seen it even without the help.

He had been dividing his attention between the ground and the branches overhead all along. What mattered was he found it.

The M-18A-1 Claymore was tied to the limbs of a tree beside the road. Its kilo of HE and deadly steel shrapnel were aimed downward for maximum burst effect. A closer inspection told him that the AP mine wasn't trip wired; it was electronically controlled. Set up at the entrance to the kill zone, it was meant to block a retreat from ambush. There would be more mines on the road farther along. Those would be trip wired and pressure activated.

The terrain ahead and to his left rose steeply, though the road remained relatively level. Bordering the road on the left side, a result of soft soil and heavy erosion, was a high, barren bluff.

The kill-zone backstop.

Barrabas circled farther left, to the back of the bluff, then crawled up to within a yard of its leading edge. He looked down and across at the opposite side of the road. Somewhere among all the profusion of plant life were the lanes of fire. From a straight-on view they were invisible. He crawled farther along the bluff top, inching his way, keeping far enough from the edge to avoid starting a disastrous landslide.

He lay there and stared for a long time, sweat streaming down his face. Even though he knew what he was looking for, he had a hell of a time seeing it. Then he caught the breaks in the branches, all at about the same height, irregularly spaced. The breaks led into tunnels bored into the brush, tunnels no more than a yard wide. It was as he'd thought. Son Ny had set up his fire lanes at sharp angles to the road so he could take targets from the side and rear. The distance from the tunnels to the far side of the road was no more than thirty-five feet. Almost point-blank. With automatic weapons it would be no contest.

Pushing back from the edge of the bluff, Barrabas took out his note pad and sketched what he had seen. He had an excellent memory, but there was no substitute for an accurate on-the-scene diagram.

Sketch done, he retraced his path down the back of the bluff and along the jungle beside the road. When he was two hundred feet from the ambush site, he crossed the road. In either direction, visibility was one-tenth of that distance. He quickly marked the track as before—three stones in a line—then moved on. Safe in the bush, he slipped out of his knapsack and canteens. He had to leave them behind, afraid that they might catch on a branch and give him away. He took a last drink of water and moved on.

When he was within fifty feet of the kill zone, he dropped to his belly again. The crawl this time was even slower; he paused every foot or two to listen, to smell, to strain his eyes against the jumble of branch outlines, vines, leaves. He was close to the back of the fire lanes. Really close. Yet he saw no one. Heard nothing. He knew they were there; he could sense them. They were well disciplined. No rustle of clothing, no whispered talk, no cigarette smoke gave their presence away. They were just sitting there, sweating like him, itching like him.

Barrabas intercepted the withdrawal route 150 feet farther on. It was a jungle trail, narrow, leaf covered, twisting back and forth between mossy man-sized boulders, which offered excellent cover for a retreat. Or a counterambush. He looked back along the trail, toward the fire lanes; he guessed the line of boulders ran all the way to the road on this side. The ambushers would be shooting from behind them.

He made another sketch, then moved up the escape trail. It was a safe bet that Son Ny's men hadn't mined or booby-trapped it. It was too easy to forget where trip wires were in a hasty evac. Although the trail was uphill, it was the easiest going he'd found so far. He dogtrotted until the dense jungle ended and the rubber trees began.

It looked like a park. The trees were all the same height and type. The brush had been cleared from around their smooth trunks. And there was room between them. Too much room. They offered little or no cover for Barrabas. He picked up his pace, wishing to hell he'd gone back for the canteens. He ran along a beaten path, ran to sunlight. The end of the grove.

From the shadow of a slender trunk he stared across the broad open space, a field slashed, burned and allowed to grow grass. Waist-high grass. He stared at the plantation house. It was a relic from British colonial days, a three-story Georgian mansion fallen into disrepair. Except for the shade trees and vines overgrowing the building proper, everything had been cleared away. The only thing that stood between him and Erika was a few hundred yards. But they were yards he could not cross. Not yet. Not alone.

The rustle of footsteps close by froze Barrabas against the tree trunk. Footsteps trailed off behind him. He could see them through the trees. Six men in camo fatigues carrying autorifles.

Where the hell did you come from? Barrabas thought. He had looked around carefully, both at the house and the field. There had been no one in sight. There had to be an explanation. And there it was: a bunker entrance, partially hidden by the base of a rubber tree. The opening was barely big enough for a man to crawl through.

The discovery answered the question that had been nagging at him: was the field mined?

Sure as shit.

The bunker was a trench dug the length of the field, shored up with poles and sandbags, covered with boards, dirt and live sod. Barrabas scowled at the small entryway. He was tempted, but the chance of coming up nose to nose with an enemy was too great. What he needed was a better view of the field and house.

After moving a good distance from the bunker, he shinnied up a tree. The long shadows cast by

fading daylight made it easier for him to see every
irregularity of terrain. There was no way anybody
could cover a trench and make it look exactly like
the surrounding ground. From the bunker a straight
line ran back to a grassy hummock close to the
mansion. The rise was too sudden to be natural. It
had all the earmarks of a machine-gun emplacement. The sod probably covered an armor plate turret with a firing port cut into it.

He moved on, circling the big house. It was almost dark by the time he finished. He had counted
four machine-gun positions, all connected by
trenches, all leading back to the house. He had
counted more than two dozen of Son Ny's soldiers.
Under a separate roof beside the mansion were
several trucks and jeeps, a tractor and a big Mercedes sedan—undoubtedly the boss's wheels.

Barrabas headed back the way he had come, or
close to it. He crossed the rubber-tree groves, then
searched for the narrow break in the bush that was
the entrance to the jungle trail. In the dim light it
was no easy task. He found a trail all right, but
could not be sure it was the right one. He moved
cautiously down it. He hadn't gone more than
twenty steps before his left foot hit wire.

There was no time to think.

At the sound of the snap, the swish, he reacted,
stepping to the side, bringing his forearms up. The
blow delivered by the spring of green bamboo
knocked him flat on his butt. It would have broken
a smaller man's arms. He looked up at the spiked

head of the bamboo whip, his heart pounding. Had he moved the other way, the cluster of fire-hardened bamboo spines would have skewered him like a fondue tidbit.

Then he heard the bell. The bell attached to the booby trap. The signal it had been sprung.

"Damn!" Barrabas growled softly.

"Over there!" someone shouted in the near distance.

"Shut up!" came an angry reply.

Barrabas had no choice now. With the wrong trail in front of him and with the enemy closing in, he had to take the hard way out. The valley. At least the mantraps would be fewer. The human-engineered mantraps, that is.

He ran to the edge of a steep slope and stopped. It was really dark down there. He started his descent in a slow, controlled way, but the ground was too steep and too slick with moss and loose leaves for him to maintain footing. He fell to his butt and slid, pushing himself along with his gloved hands, trying to put as much distance as possible between himself and his pursuers. When he reached a gully it came as a real shock. The bottom just dropped out, and he fell onto a pile of boulders and stream rubble. He sat there, listening. They were coming. They were moving with more care than he had, but they were coming just the same.

Barrabas knew the dangers of going farther down. The moss carpet could conceal chasms forty feet deep. There could be water obstacles, rivers, streams too fast for him to cross. He had to stay where he was, evade them in the dark until they gave up the search.

He felt his way along the deep U-shaped gully, trying to move both quickly and quietly. It was as impossible for him as it was for those who chased him. A sound ahead made him stop dead. Somebody was coming up toward him. They had cut him off. Whoever these guys were, they were good. They knew all the ways out and exactly how to cover them. They wanted to drive him down the hill, to trap him against some natural barrier he could not get past. Then, even in the pitch dark, they could tighten the noose, find and kill him.

Since there was no place to go, Barrabas went nowhere. He took a position beside a fallen log that stuck out over the edge of the gully on the sloping side. In the dark only the silvery sheen of the moss on its upper surface could be seen. He pulled off his gloves and stuffed them in a back pocket. He made sure his feet were solidly planted, then he relaxed. He breathed slowly and evenly, listening to the shuffle, the clatter of the man coming at him. He could feel the distance narrowing. In his mind he formed a picture of what was going to happen.

Then he made it come true.

Simultaneously, he reached out with his left hand, grabbing a sweaty shoulder, and swung with his right, across his chest. From the height of the shoulder he knew where his target would be.

The soldier let out a small, soft noise that was cut

off by the edge of a hand crushing his windpipe.

Barrabas caught the suffocating merc from behind, holding him by the armpits, and hauled him up out of the gully. The man did not try to attack him; he was too busy clawing at his own collapsed airway. Barrabas took his weapon, a CAR-15, and his canteen and left him on the mossy bed to writhe his final seconds away.

The white-haired man jumped back into the gully and moved quickly downhill. When he had put a good distance between himself and the hard contact, Barrabas stopped, sat down on a boulder and opened the man's canteen. He sniffed its contents and muttered a curse. It wasn't water; it was soda pop. Sri Lankan soda pop. Nauseatingly sweet, it had no distinct flavor. It smelled like cheap rose perfume. He popped a handful of salt tabs and forced himself to drink deep. Liquid was liquid.

He leaned back against the gully's bank and shut his eyes. Until first light, there was nothing to do but wait.

12

T.M. returned to the tiny back bedroom where his family was hiding. He could not conceal his concern from them. It was in his face, in his eyes.

"What is it?" Niramala asked.

"The police were just here," he said, then corrected himself. "No, not just the police. Sergeant Perara."

T.M.'s wife stiffened in her chair.

"He's leading an antiterrorist unit searching the Muslim quarter for escaped Eelam Tigers. Going door to door. Our friends managed to keep him from going through the whole house, but they think he knows we are here. He asked about us specifically."

"Why doesn't he leave us alone?!" Jenny said, practically in tears. "What does he want?"

T.M. knew, but did not answer. The Sinhalese policeman wanted to take everything he had. His money, his property, his life and those he loved. He wanted to take it all because he had the power to do it.

Niramala knew, too. She put an arm around her daughter's shoulders.

"I told Barrabas I would direct his men to the

plantation in Matale tomorrow,'' T.M. went on. "I must go. I have no choice. I must help save Erika. As soon as I've done what I promised, I will return and we will find shelter elsewhere.''

"What if something happens while you're gone?" Niramala said. "What can we do? Where can we go?''

T.M. picked up the sawed-off shotgun and ammo bag and handed it to his son. "Godfrey," he said, "until I get back, you are the protector of our family. If the police come again and try to get in, take your mother and sisters out the back window. Go back to the Netherlands Imports building. It's been badly burned, so you must be very careful when you enter. Part of it could collapse. In the warehouse, at the rear wall, there are some empty unburned crates. Hide in them until I come for you. Use the gun only if you absolutely must, but remember, your target has to be close, very close.''

"I remember," Godfrey said.

T.M. managed a smile for his brave son. He trusted the boy. It was fate he did not trust. Not in the light of recent events. He put his arms around Godfrey and Niramala; his daughters put theirs around him.

"Everything is going to be all right," he said with more conviction than he felt.

WALKER JESSUP covered the untouched filet mignon with his paper napkin.

"Aren't you going to eat that?" Lopez said hopefully from the seat at his right.

Jessup pushed the loaded airline dinner tray onto the Mexican American's fold-down table.

"You on a diet?" Lopez asked, using a plastic knife to saw through two-and-a-half-inches of prime beef.

The plastic blade cut the wonderfully rare meat like a razor. It was that tender. Jessup looked away from the spectacle. "Yeah, a diet," he said to the wiry guy.

"Too bad. This is one great steak."

The sound of disappearing filet was as annoying to Jessup as the sight. He picked up his earphone headset and put it on, adjusting the channel selector to some laid-back jazz. He cranked up the volume until it drowned out the lip-smacking enjoyment to his right. Tightly wedged into an aisle seat, he could see most of the interior of the 727. It was deserted. A plane designed to carry two hundred was ferrying six. Compliments of the CIA.

The SOBs hadn't given him any trouble, not yet, anyway. He had seriously underestimated O'Toole's abilities as a team leader. Once he'd realized what the situation was, the Irishman had straightened up and taken charge. He kept a tight rein on his troops, too, allowing them no in-flight booze, not even wine with dinner. O'Toole knew firsthand how quickly one drinkie-poo could lead to another.

Jessup's estimations of some of the other mercenaries were closer to target. Nanos and William Starfoot II, a.k.a. Billy Two, were, if anything, wilder than their dossiers had let on. Dossiers only listed the things they had been caught at. Lopez was an operator, too, but a successful one. If he had applied his natural talents, he could have actually made it in the real world—as, say, a coke runner from Bogotá to Key West. If Nanos and Billy Two had tried something like that, they'd have found some way to screw it up, most likely with floozies. With them, it was always floozies.

Nate Beck was an oddball. Slight of build, narrow shouldered, intellectual, he did not fit the standard double-Y-chromosome mold of a soldier of fortune. To Jessup's way of thinking, Beck was the second craziest of the lot.

First prize went to the three hundred pounds of nut case firmly wedged into an aisle seat. The guy in the XXL camouflage safari shirt from the big and tall shop. The guy whose stomach was growling up a storm while he sipped unsweetened iced tea. Jessup himself.

The Texan thought about what was going to happen once they touched down in Colombo. His mission with the SOBs. His mission alone. If the bad guys didn't kill him, there was a good chance that Barrabas would.

He looked over at Lopez, who was mopping up steak juice with a chunk of parkerhouse roll. If I live through this, he promised himself, I'm going to eat New York.

13

Through the sweltering jungle night Barrabas faded in and out, asleep, awake at the fall of a leaf, asleep again. He tried not to think about the assault the next day, tried not to consciously begin to plan. The details needed time to sit in his mind, to filter through.

He thought—or dreamed—a lot about Erika. About the old days.

When they had first met on the beach at Vung Tau, he had been working on a second dozen half-liter bottles of La Rue "Tiger" beer, the B-40 empties tipped brown bottoms up and stuck in the sand around him. At the moment the tall, tanned blonde in the skimpy black bikini stopped to talk, the rewards for heroism above and beyond, for playing the paper game, were all still his. The dates with the Saigon society girls, spoiled daughters of generals and ambassadors. The private office in the MACV building. The respect of Saigon's maître d's and headwaiters. But the tang had long gone.

He had known for years that the system was corrupt, but he thought he could make a difference. One man. That he could win his own scaled-down war despite everything the system threw at him. He had been wrong. There were some things that couldn't be fought, that had to be walked away from.

He had lost people he loved in Vietnam. Americans, of course. But Vietnamese, too. Peasants he had helped and who had helped him. They had been like anybody else with roots in the soil, like farmers and ranchers he had known back in Wyoming. More concerned about rainfall and fertilizer than politics. Only his friends, the villagers, had been stuck in the middle of hell, waiting to see which side won, trying to survive the affections and angers of both. It was a war of PR as well as mortar rounds. Barrabas had tried to wage it with a human face, a caring face. The VC legal cadre living among and terrorizing the uncommitted peasants had to be identified, arrested and neutralized. With the co-operation of the people, Barrabas had proved that it could be done.

The collapse of Operation Achilles had ended many things for him. His naiveté. His ambition as a career Army officer. His interest in the female offspring of generals. Erika Dykstra had come along at just the right time for him.

Ten years later he could still talk to her and know she understood, still take comfort in the lush contours of her body. She never criticized his drinking or his edge-of-hell life-style. Those things were givens, had been givens on the wide sandy beach so long ago.

He thought about the danger she was now in and caught himself. Fury had no purpose yet. It was only a drain on his reserve of strength. He closed his mind to everything but the night sounds around him. The drip of moisture from leaf to leaf to leaf. The skittering of tiny feet through the branches overhead. The groan of tree limbs rubbing.

And he dozed.

And he dreamed.

A soldier's dream. Of another night. In another jungle. Not alone in the smothering darkness, but back to back with the man the villagers named Sergeant Mercy. The same man the VC knew as Executioner. The man he called Sarge.

Their scouting party had been cut off by an enemy advance and pursued and harassed until only the two of them were left, surrounded now by North Vietnamese regulars, who, though they could not be seen, could not see them, either. But they were close enough to spit on.

No words passed between the two big men. They both knew they couldn't shoot. The muzzle-flashes of their M-16s would betray their position and bring on a horrendous cross fire. Both knew what had to be done. They put down their assault rifles and took up grenades, pulling the pins, waiting for a sound to give away their attackers.

As they sat there and sweated, Barrabas thought he could feel the sarge's heart pounding right through his back, through the combined layers of their flak vests. But he couldn't be sure it wasn't his own. Pumped was not the word for what he felt.

Then there was a thud off to the right. An enemy grenade. Barrabas and the sarge curled and covered, putting the backs of their flak vests to the explosion.

The sarge sat up and threw. The crump of the blast was followed by a piercing shriek of pain. And a rustle of movement. Barrabas let the spoon pop free and tossed at the sound, not twenty-five feet away. Another blast. Followed by more screams.

The two Americans curled and covered again. Frag grenades sailed through the branches overhead. And once again the air was full of singing metal.

The enemy was throwing long.

But the Americans had tigers' eyes. They made every grenade count. Barrabas could feel the growing confusion and terror in the NVA around them. He could feel the steel circle that held them trapped begin to tremble and come apart.

The sarge touched his arm and crawled away to the left.

Barrabas followed. He, too, could smell the weak link, the clear space.

In his dream, Barrabas had the same warming thought he had had fifteen years before: he visualized the NVA waiting until dawn, until they could see the men they thought they had trapped, and finding only their own dead and grenade craters blown into the soft red earth. Had they been chasing shadows?

Rain woke Barrabas. It pelted his head and shoulders. He tipped up his face and let it wash over him, remembering the dream, remembering John Macklin Bolan. The sarge had gone his own way long ago.

A personal and private war against the Mafia. They said he was dead. Barrabas knew better.

Shadows can't be killed.

Light was breaking through the jungle canopy overhead. Barrabas stretched.

It was time to go to war.

BARRABAS WAS SITTING IN THE SHADE, upwind of the coconut-softening pond when the three-car caravan drove up. As the occupants of the cars began getting out, he rose and walked over to them, CAR-15 slung over his shoulder.

"Sorry it took us so long to get here, Colonel," O'Toole said as he shook his hand. "The traffic back in Colombo was unreal."

"Yeah," Nanos said, "survival of the fittest. The bigger the car, the more rights the driver's got."

Barrabas stared at Jessup, who was struggling to get out of the back seat of the middle car. "What the fuck are you doing here?" he demanded.

The fat man's face showed signs of borderline heat prostration. His breathing was shallow and fast. The sudden change in climate had really hit him hard.

"It's a long story," Jessup said, pulling out a handkerchief and mopping his dripping face and neck. "We came up short on personnel at the last minute. I couldn't get in contact with Dr. Hatton and Hayes on Majorca."

Barrabas scowled. They were two soldiers who would be sorely missed. Dr. Lee Hatton was a combat doctor par excellence; she was also a skilled hand-to-hand fighter. Claude Hayes was a jungle veteran, having fought in Africa with his black brothers in various liberation struggles there. Jessup made up for the two of them in volume, but from the way he looked, he wasn't going to be worth much in battle.

"You picked a bad one to come along on," Barrabas told the Texan. "We've got a lot of ground to cover and this is as cool as it gets around here."

Jessup gave him a weak smile. "No problem," he said.

"What kind of weapons did you bring?"

Nanos and Billy Two opened the trunk of the Taunus sedan, the lead car. "Chicom ordnance, Colonel," Billy Two said, holding up a Type 56 AK with 30-round magazine.

"You got all that stuff through customs?" Barrabas asked.

"No," Jessup said, lumbering slowly into the shade. "A contact of mine knows somebody high up in the military here. Through him we picked up some captured Eelam Tiger guns. This Sri Lankan officer also gave us a name we could use to get through the checkpoints without being searched."

Barrabas nodded. "If we leave a few AKs behind, the authorities will think terrorists hit the plantation. They get the blame for everything here. No reason why they shouldn't take the heat for this, too." He walked over to the softening pond, unslung the captured CAR and tossed the weapon in.

"We brought some handguns into the country with us," Beck said, offering Barrabas a Browning Hi-Power in a black web holster.

The white-haired man slid the automatic out and looked at it critically.

"I know it's not yours," Jessup said, "but it's been reworked by an expert."

Barrabas released the clip, checked to see that it was fully loaded, then reinserted it. He turned back to the pool. He liked the nonslip neoprene wraparound grips. Even with sweaty palms they afforded a secure hold. He cocked the pistol, raised it and opened fire on the floating coconut hulls. Head-sized targets shattered under the hail of 9mm lead. He emptied the 13-round magazine in short order. "Nice trigger job."

"Four pounds of pull," Jessup said. "Your specs."

Barrabas accepted a fresh clip from Beck, replaced the empty and started to buckle on the belt and holster.

T.M., who had been standing beside the cars, blending in with the paint jobs, stepped up and said, "I must talk to you."

Barrabas locked the belt buckle, putting the 9mm automatic on his left hip, butt first for right-handed cross draw. "Shoot," he said.

"I can't stay and help you any further. I'm sorry, but my family is in some danger back in Colombo. That police sergeant...."

"You mean Perara?"

"Yes, I think he's still after me. Us. And I'm afraid he's discovered where we have been hiding. I must return and move my family to a safer place."

Barrabas felt like telling him that he shouldn't have come, that he should have seen to his own first, but he didn't. Erika was as much a part of T.M.'s family as Jenny or Sheila. T.M. had done what he had to do. The honorable thing.

"How will we be able to find you after you move?" Barrabas asked.

"My Muslim friends will know where we have gone."

"Go on, then, get back to your family. Don't worry about it. You've already helped us plenty."

"Good luck," T.M. said, and he got into the last car in the line, backed it up and roared back the way they had come.

"A tough little cookie," Jessup said.

"Yeah," Barrabas said, joining him in the shade. He watched as his SOBs unloaded the gear from the cars. If they were suffering from the heat and humidity, they didn't let it show.

"Hey, Lopez," Nanos said, sniffing at the air, "don't it make you hungry for a big slice of coconut pie?"

"Or a handful of macaroons?" Billy Two added.

"Hey, I'm never gonna eat coconut again," the Mexican American said. "*Dios*, does this place stink!"

"Snap it up," O'Toole told them. "Less chatter, more motion."

When they had checked all the weapons and inventoried ammo, Barrabas diagramed the plantation in the dirt. He pointed out the four machine-gun positions, their arcs of fire, and the connecting trenches. Then he drew the ambush setup and withdrawal route.

"If this operation is going to work," he said, "we have to be in their faces before they know what hit them. That means two things. We do this by the numbers. Synchronized. Precise. It also means we split up. Liam, you, Billy Two and Nanos in one group. Me, Lopez and Beck in the other."

"Aren't you forgetting somebody?" Jessup said.

"I'll get to you in a minute. We're going to take both cars down the dirt track. At the marker for the first ground sensor, we'll start running them bumper to bumper. I mean, touching."

"To confuse the sensors," O'Toole said. "If there's no separation between sets of wheels, it'll register as one vehicle."

"Right. We run that way to the marker I left for the ambush site. There the six of us will get out and work quickly around behind the firing lanes to the escape route. Liam, Billy and Nanos, you'll set up shop there. Get into position to take out the ambush team as they pull back. Lopez, Beck and I will continue up the trail to the tunnel, penetrate it and take out the machine gun on top. Both groups will hit at the same time."

"You still haven't gotten to me," Jessup said.

"You're the signal," Barrabas told him. "After we leave you at the ambush marker, you drive the lead car another hundred feet, aiming it down the middle of the road. Then you stop, get out and drop a rock on the gas pedal. When the car rolls over the AP mines at the other end of the kill zone, everybody has the green light."

"And after that?" Jessup asked. "Do you want me to come up the trail and help out?"

Barrabas considered the size of the tunnel entrance and the size of the Texan. No way. "Stay with the operational car. Make sure nobody gets away down the road."

Jessup grimaced, but said nothing.

"My group," Barrabas went on, "is responsible for the two MGs on the back side of the house. Liam, your guys will negate the other two MG positions and enter the house from the front." He looked at his watch. "It's 6:20 P.M. now. We hit 'em in about ten minutes."

"We've got to do this while there's still some daylight, huh?" Nanos wondered aloud.

"Only if you want to live through it," Barrabas told him. "It's Booby Trap City up there."

"I want to live through it," Nanos said. "Did I tell you, I got a new lady in San Francisco?"

Barrabas glanced at O'Toole who, behind the Greek's back, twirled his upraised index finger in the air. The universal "whoopee" sign, delivered with feeble enthusiasm.

"Another Stanford graduate, I suppose?"

"No, Colonel, she's a professional entertainer—an ecdysiast—"

"Uh, Alex," Beck cut in, "I hate to tell you but that isn't quite true. An ecdysiast, strictly speaking, is a stripper."

"Yeah, that's right, Nanos," Lopez chimed in, his glee undisguised. "Your new sweetbuns didn't take anything off that I noticed. How 'bout you, Billy? Did you see anything hit the stage after she stepped out?"

"Only your chin and mine," the Indian said.

"Holy shit! I think you guys are actually jealous."

"Nope," O'Toole told the Greek, "just long-suffering. Shall we go, gentlemen?"

The SOBs and Jessup piled into the pair of cars, with Liam driving the last, a four-door Datsun, and Barrabas taking the lead Taunus. The white-haired man put the automatic sedan into Drive and turned down the two-rut road. The fringe of grass growing up between the ruts made a steady rasping sound on the car's undercarriage. They were riding low in back. Really low.

Barrabas looked up into the rearview mirror and saw only Jessup. The fat guy had the whole back seat to himself. In the side mirror he could see Liam steering the white Datsun through the dust cloud he was kicking up. He knew why the SOBs were along. Because he needed them. Because he had asked. It was the kind of job any one of them would have done free for the others. Why Walker Jessup was risking his life was a mystery. He shut the thought out of his mind and concentrated on the track ahead. Palm fronds, banana leaves, tree limbs were smacking the windshield, brushing the side of the car. He had to slow down to make out the road.

When the three rocks came into view, he stopped, rolled down his window and motioned for O'Toole to pull up closer. Barrabas kept his foot on the brake. When the cars hit, the Datsun's front bumper climbed up over the Taunus's rear, locking in place. Barrabas waved again, feathering the brakes. O'Toole gave the Datsun some gas and, with a shriek of metal on metal, the two cars rolled forward.

By working the brakes, Barrabas maintained contact with the Datsun. On the first sharp turn, the pressure point shifted along the Taunus's rear end, and taillights and turn signals shattered. There was nothing but silence in the car. Barrabas stole a quick glance at Lopez. The wiry guy had his Chinese assault rifle angled out the passenger window, ready to rip. No more wisecracks. No more jive. From here on out, it was all business.

As the second set of markers came up, Barrabas ground the brake pedal to the floorboards. Both cars stopped amid the smell of burning brake pads. He jumped out and hurried to help Nanos free the Datsun's bumper. Once that was done, he accepted a Kalashnikov and extra magazines from Lopez. The spare mags he stuck under the web belt at the small of his back.

"Set your watches," he told his men. And when they were ready he said, "Mark! Four minutes from now, Jessup does a number on the car."

He waved for the SOBs to follow and slipped through the wall of green on the right side of the road. Four minutes wasn't a lot of time to cover the ground they had to cover. They had to move quietly and quickly. On their bellies for most of the way. Every tree root, every vine that tugged at them was an enemy, a potential betrayer. Barrabas knew the guys had to be hurting now. He was hurting. The sweat boiled off him as he furiously crawled through the bush.

When he reached the trail, he took cover behind a mossy boulder and checked the time. Two and a half minutes had gone by. They were going to have to run the last leg. Uphill. He gestured to O'Toole, indicating the direction the retreating ambushers would be coming from, then waved Lopez and Beck on. He raced up the trail, jumping the smaller rocks, the twisted, buttressed tree trunks. He couldn't hear the others behind him; the beating of his own heart, the rasping of his own breath was too loud in his ears.

Ahead there was more light. Another jarring twenty-five strides and he broke into the rubber-tree groves. The AK gripped between his hands seemed to weigh a hundred pounds instead of ten, but he kept on running. The fury so long bottled up, the fury over the past as well as the present, was bubbling over, driving him to his physical limits.

When he saw the tunnel entrance, he slowed, letting Lopez and Beck catch up. All three reached the opening at the same time.

"You guys okay?"

Red faced, panting, bathed in sweat, Beck said, "Fine. Just give me a second."

Barrabas looked at his watch. "I'll give you ten."

JESSUP ROLLED THE HEAVY STONE onto the Taunus's floorboards, then straightened up, groaning. Seventy-five feet dead ahead was the kill zone, just as the colonel had described it: on his left the sheer wall of the bluff, on the right the heavy jungle and concealed lanes of fire.

He fished out his handkerchief, wrung it between his hands, then mopped his face. Things hadn't worked out according to plan. He hadn't foreseen the devastating effects of heat and humidity on a man eighty pounds overweight. It had been vanity. He'd kidded himself into thinking that the climate would only slow him down. There were going to be some mighty unhappy fellows back at Langley, but he didn't give a goddamn. He knew how he felt. He felt as if he was going to die. Every breath was an effort.

There was still a slim chance that he could do the job he'd been sent to do. He was blocking the only road out. All he needed was some luck.

He slid the Combat Colt out of shoulder leather, cocked and locked it, then eased it back. He checked his watch. It was time. He leaned over the driver's seat, jerked up on the hand brake as hard as he could, then dropped the car into gear. As he flattened the accelerator with the rock, the four-cylinder wailed in protest.

Jessup tapped in the release button at the end of the hand brake. Then he jumped back as the lever snapped down, as the car surged forward.

He didn't watch it go. He hurried toward the cover of the rear of the Datsun, drawing the Colt, thumbing down its safety as he lumbered along.

A little luck, he told himself, puffing from the strain. Just a little luck.

MACATEE LISTENED to the silence in his headset with growing alarm. He was the ambush leader. He sat with two men on his left, three on his right, connected to them by lengths of clear monofilament fishing line looped loosely around their fingers. Macatee was hooked up to the string of ground sensors by the apparatus on his head. He had already given his men the single hard tug on the line that meant the target was approaching. The sensors had been ticking off the approach of the lone car with clockwork precision; then they had stopped. That meant the vehicle had stopped. Closeby.

Come on, you morons, he thought, itching all over, itching to use the CAR-15 in his fist. The sooner they wasted the rescue team, the sooner the spoils would get divvied up. The spoils being one hot blonde. Party time.

A smile spread over his face as the ground sensors

once again registered movement on the road. Maybe the suckers had had a bit of car trouble? He tucked the CAR-15's adjustable stock hard into the hollow of his shoulder and rested nearly a half foot of flash hider on a cleft in the rock in front of him.

The little sedan leaped into his green tunnel of view, hit the line of AP mines and jumped. The flat double whump blew the front end six feet off the ground. It twisted as it dropped, the spinning right rear wheel catching first and flipping the car onto its side, roof turned toward the ambush.

Macatee tightened down on the trigger and the stubby autocarbine obediently bucked and barked. There was a lot of barking going on. From the six weapons 5.56mm tumblers stitched front and back windows, slashed through the roof. Macatee unloaded a 40-round mag before he realized something was wrong.

He could see through the frosted ruin of the front windshield. No body hung suspended from the steering wheel. No body slumped against the passenger door. With a sudden, sick feeling in the pit of his stomach, he jerked the fishing line laid across his lap.

He jerked it twice.

The retreat signal.

They had been had. In spades.

Macatee was the first man out of the chute, swapping a full CAR mag for the empty on the run, sprinting up the narrow trail between the boulders. They would make it. His guys were good. And they knew the routine inside out. As he pushed the CAR's bolt release, his foot clipped a root and he stumbled. He stumbled, swearing, just as the trap was sprung.

Even as Macatee fell behind a rock, autorifle fire from both sides of the trail slammed into boulders, tree trunks and men. The cross fire had been perfectly timed to catch the most targets between available cover. He looked back and saw three of his men down; two were already doing the dance; the third, the man closest to him, was lying on his back, blowing bubbles from a sucking chest wound.

He knew he had to move now, while the others were still drawing fire. He scrambled to a low crouch, jumped out from behind the rock and came instantly face-to-face with a short, stocky red-haired guy in fatigues and camo warpaint.

At least this one is dead, he thought, squeezing the CAR's trigger.

Before the hammer dropped, there was a screech of steel on steel as the red-haired guy jabbed with his AK's unfolded spike bayonet, deflecting the midchest point of aim. Macatee's crisp, 6-round burst ravaged only the shrubbery.

That put him one step behind.

And there was no time to play catch-up.

The metal-shod butt of the AK smashed the side of his head. A flash of white-hot pain followed a heartbeat later by another, deeper and more terrible hurt. A combination of pressure and searing pain that drove him to his knees.

Instinctively, he clutched at the muzzle and sights of the AK, trying to pull the long cruciform bayonet from his bowels. He knew what was coming. But nothing in his experience could have prepared him for the impossible agony as the AK muzzle spat flame between his hands.

14

"Why so nervous, Karl?" Son Ny asked. "I keep telling you there's nothing to worry about. It's a Chinese finger trap, remember?"

Heiss stopped pacing and stared at the major general who sat in a big wingback chair, in safari shirt and matching shorts, hands laced behind his greasy head, his boots and knee-sock clad legs crossed and propped up on an ottoman; he was the grinning picture of confidence. This while Heiss's confidence was seriously on the wane; decent rations, a clean bed and daily baths were weakening Heiss's resolve. Though it pained Heiss to admit it, Son Ny had been right. The strains of his African imprisonment had affected his mind. With the return of strength and health, Heiss's mental powers had also come back. The most important of these was memory. Then came judgment.

Heiss remembered how it had been in the good old days a decade before. He remembered exactly. The major general had been an officer in the ARVN twenty-fifth division. The twenty-fifth was the only unit in the republic someone like Son Ny could have risen to authority in. It was notorious for its cowards and criminals. Son Ny had certainly been qualified to push heroin to desperate, homesick GIs, especially with all the protection he could buy from his corrupt countrymen. He might even have been qualified to run an international hatchet squad. But as a tactician, he was no Karl Heiss. And he certainly was no Nile Barrabas.

"I want a gun," Heiss told him.

Son Ny gave him a quizzical, faintly amused look.

"A gun of my own to carry. You do have an extra pistol, don't you?"

The major general rose reluctantly, as if placating a stubborn child. He walked over to the desk, opened the center drawer and took out two weapons in holsters. One was a blue steel Smith & Wesson revolver, a Chiefs Special in .38 caliber. The other was a nickel-plated U.S. Government Model Colt Automatic. The .45 had mother-of-pearl grips.

Heiss looked at the pair of guns on the desk blotter. "Do I get to guess which one's mine?"

Son Ny shoved the little revolver at him.

Heiss picked up the gun and pulled it from its clip-on belt holster. He swung out the cylinder to make sure it was loaded, then snapped it back and replaced the handgun in its sheath. As he clipped the weapon to his waistband, he watched Son Ny shrug into the .45 auto's shoulder harness.

"Feel more comfortable now?" the major general asked.

The answer, unspoken, was no.

Tension still gripped Heiss by the throat. How could he feel at ease when the man in charge was the Peter Principle in action?

"Are you afraid Barrabas won't come before the deadline's up?" Son Ny asked as he drew his gleaming pimp's gun, jacked a live round under the firing pin and let the hammer down. "It'll be a different sort of game after we kill his woman. He'll be the hunter then. Just think, Karl, you'll be looking over your shoulder for that white head of hair for the rest of your life."

Heiss said nothing. Son Ny had it completely wrong. He was afraid Barrabas would show. That he would fall like rolling thunder on the deluded egomaniac's "finger trap."

"At least you will have had some revenge," Son Ny said.

It was not enough for Heiss. He wanted Barrabas dead but he wanted to survive the experience, to savor it well into his dotage.

The conversation was interrupted by distant explosions, then a sustained crackle of small-arms fire.

"So, Karl, you're going to have your trophy, after all," Son Ny said. "Oh, ye of little faith. . . ."

Heiss hurried to a window. Beyond the cleared area he could see nothing but trees. The shooting stopped as suddenly as it had begun.

"What a tiny fuss!" the major general remarked. "Our friend Barrabas didn't put up much of a fight. I'm disappointed. I'd hoped at least he'd give my men a proper workout."

The shooting started up again. But it was different. The bursts of autofire were shorter, and the reports themselves more muffled.

"Somebody is putting up a fight," Heiss said coldly. "A one-sided fight from what I can hear."

Son Ny joined him at the window. "It sounds like AKs to me," he said. "But where's the answering fire? Why aren't they shooting back?"

Heiss grimaced. "You do have an escape plan, I presume?"

Though the major general's eyes were hidden behind sunglasses, the reaction was there on his face just the same. Below the pencil mustache, his sensual lips compressed into a narrow, carmine gash. "Of course I have an escape plan," he said, "but it's a bit premature to be considering—"

"What about the girl?" Heiss said. "What do we do with her if your wonderful defense plan falls apart?"

"Kill her, certainly. And leave the corpse for Barrabas to find. A shame not to enjoy her first, but if worse comes to worst, it can't be helped. I'll do the job myself, if you're squeamish."

Heiss shook his head. "I'm not squeamish."

NATE BECK didn't volunteer to be first man into the covered trench because he was a glory hound. He went first because he was claustrophobic. Because it was first or not at all. At least that way there would be two guys behind to push him if he froze up partway along.

The tunnel was so dark he couldn't see a yard in front of his face. It smelled musty and damp, like freshly turned earth. There was enough room for him to squirm along, but he had to keep his head down or bump it on the boards above. He crawled with the AK resting on top of his arms. There was no light ahead, no end in sight and as he moved deeper and deeper, he lost his sense of direction; he couldn't tell if he was crawling uphill or down. He was suffocated by the darkness, by the closeness of floor, walls, ceiling. The covered trench was like a coffin one hundred yards long.

Despite his fear, he kept moving.

If mama could only see me now, he thought. Scared out of my goddamn mind, but doing it anyway. She'd have heart failure. She'd have me put under psychiatric observation for my own good.

In the Becks' middle-class Jewish household, a confrontation with danger had consisted of eating fish for dinner. There were all those deadly little bones to be wary of. And his mother sat at his elbow counting the number of times he chewed each bite, making sure the fish had melted into an unrecognizable pulp in his mouth before she would allow him to swallow. According to family tradition, one could also strangle to death on the little white squirmy thing attached to the yolk of a raw egg. It was scrupulously removed on the tines of a fork before the egg was cooked and consigned to the garbage pail with a Yiddish curse.

There had been other irrational fears and superstitions, dealing with travel by air or sea, the use of public lavatories, strenuous exercise, sexual contact. Old-country notions. Like the innate joys of suffering. Martyrdom. Guilt.

These quaint guidelines for living produced, on the whole, nice, polite men who shaved every day, smelled good and wore suits. If, heaven forbid, they were ever shot at, they wouldn't even consider shooting back. They wouldn't know how. Outside the legally constituted armed forces and the police, only Nazis and crooks had guns. Guns were for goyim. So were Errol Flynn and John Wayne, his boyhood idols.

As a youngster Nate Beck had always felt like a traitor to his people because he liked guns and swashbucklers. And no matter what anybody said, guilt was no fun.

If his mama could see him now, he knew exactly what she would say: "See? See where it's all gotten you? Thirty-three years old and already a dead man. And who's to blame? Not your mother! Your mother warned you. But would you listen?"

Ahead, it was definitely getting lighter. Beck picked up the pace. He didn't care about the danger before him. He wanted out of the damned tunnel. Fast.

When he reached the end, he forced himself to hang back, to stay in the shadows inside the opening. "I'm going to hit the MG," he told Barrabas and Lopez. His voice sounded funny to him. High-pitched. Squeaky. He hoped to God the Mickey Mouse impression was a figment, not a fact.

Blushing to the tips of his ears, Beck slithered out

of the covered trench to within fifteen yards of the plantation house. As he lay on his belly, the MG position was to his right, a manmade mound camouflaged with sod. He could see the glint of metal between the cracks in the sections of grass-covered dirt. There was no firing port on the backside of the turret. Below the raised mound was another narrow, wood-framed opening in the ground, the entrance to the emplacement.

He thought briefly about going in that way and knew he couldn't do it. Though Nate admitted to being a trifle neurotic, suicidal he wasn't. As he stared at the MG turret he had a flash of insight. Ventilation. The fumes and gases of sustained full-auto fire could knock a guy out, or even kill him. There had to be a vent. It had to be on top.

Beck jumped to his feet and ran to the back of the emplacement. The metal cylinder was only half roofed over, half covered with sod. He could see heads inside.

The heads could see him.

"Jesus!" one of the MG team cried, grabbing his mini-Uzi.

Beck did what Big John, what Errol, would have done. He gritted his teeth, jammed the AK's muzzle into the pit and pinned the trigger. The steel cylinder acted like a megaphone, compressing, projecting the deafening clatter of six hundred rounds per minute. It also compressed the humanity within. Which was a good thing because Beck was too pumped to consider the danger of lead-on-steel deflections. The packed bodies inside the turret soaked up 7.62x39mm slugs without regard to their source. Straight-on hits, ricochets, bank shots were all the same to them.

It was over in three seconds.

For Nate it was almost over for good. Standing beside the turret he was an easy target for the lone rifleman at the MG position on the other rear corner of the house. An instant before a volley of slugs slashed the air at belly height, Beck's legs were cut out from under him. He and Barrabas hit the dirt in a pile.

"Thanks, Colonel," he said as he squirmed for cover behind the turret.

"That was dumb work, Beck, but nicely done."

Nate wasn't sure it was meant as a compliment until he saw the grin on Barrabas's face.

More bullets whined overhead, clanging off the steel cylinder. Beck discarded the empty magazine and cracked in a fresh one.

The white-haired man pointed at the entrance to the captured machine-gun nest. "Inside there's another tunnel. It connects this MG with the one that guy's using for cover. Beck, get your tail down there and plug up the exit. Lopez, lay down some covering fire for me. I'm going to go turn that guy off."

Beck slipped through the turret entrance, shoving aside dangling rubber arms and legs to get at the opening to the tunnel. He was twenty-five feet down the passage, surrounded by suffocating darkness before he realized it. The colonel's praise had gone to his head and then some. It had made him feel like a lion. Now the lion was back in Neurosis City.

Here we go again, he told himself, crawling like a madman through the narrow shaft.

Inside the tunnel the staccato bursts of gunfire raging between the two turrets were muffled. At least, he thought, there was no way the MG positions could pour .308-caliber slugs at each other. Though their arcs of fire overlapped at the tree line, at the corners of the house their swing was no more than 110 degrees.

Beck estimated that he was more than halfway along, but he could still see no light from the other end. Was the way out sealed off? Was he going to have to back crawl to get the hell out?

He moved very cautiously the next forty feet. Then he saw something. He was four feet away when he realized that what he was looking at were the soles of a man's boots. One of the MG team had backed into the tunnel and was lying in wait.

Beck's shocked expulsion of breath wasn't loud, but it was loud enough to alert the man in front of him.

"Shit!" the merc growled, squirming, twisting in the tight passage, working his right hand down between his legs.

Beck felt an instant of pure panic. There was absolutely no place for him to go.

The heavy-caliber handgun boomed over and

over, muzzle-flashes lighting up the tunnel. Beck rolled to his side, pressing his back to the wall. His opponent was hampered by his own legs and rear end. Beck was not. He flattened the AK's trigger and hung on as the assault rifle chugged and rattled, fountaining spent brass. Multiple hits with steel-cored slugs put a quick end to the squirming in front of him.

Nate lay there, gasping, coughing, eyes tearing from the trapped cordite smoke.

The firefight above peaked, then faded to nothing. Beck wiped stinging eyes with the back of his hand. He opened them in time to see the body before him start to move.

"Oh, Lord, no!" he groaned, fumbling with the AK's magazine release, fumbling with the empty clip.

The man in front of him disappeared. Light flooded the end of the tunnel.

Beck slammed in a full mag, yanked back the operating handle and sighted down the center of the passage.

"You all right, Nate?"

It was Lopez.

ERIKA WATCHED IN SPELLBOUND HORROR as the room disintegrated around her. Automatic-rifle fire crashed through the windows, shattering lamps, vases, chewing up a wall full of books in leather bindings. Tied to the massive chair, she was unable to drop to the floor, unable to duck. All she could do was avert her face and pray. Outside the closed door to the library, men were running, cursing.

Barrabas had come for her as she had known he would. And he was hurting them. That he could beat Son Ny's mercenaries was never in doubt. The real question was, if he beat them, would Heiss and Son Ny let him win? Would they let her live?

The door to the library swung inward.

Erika was about to find out.

"Go on, do it!" Son Ny told Heiss. "Do it and let's get the hell out!"

Despite her precarious position, or perhaps because of it, Erika took great pleasure in seeing the major general on the hurting end of the stick. All his posing, his bluster, was gone now; he was showing his true colors. She remembered a famous bit of Saigon graffiti: "The Vietnamese flag is well designed; where they're not red, they're yellow." It fitted Son Ny like a Bill Blass body bag.

Heiss said nothing, did nothing. He just stood there, staring, with the snub-nosed revolver in his hand.

"If you think I'm going to wait around while you milk this for all it's worth, you're insane," Son Ny said. The Vietnamese turned on his heel and left.

Erika knew what was about to happen. Heiss was going to have his revenge on Barrabas after all, have it by blowing her head off. It was a cleaner finish than the one Son Ny had planned for her. At least there would be no humiliation, no degradation.

Heiss stepped up beside her and shoved the cold Smith & Wesson snout hard against her temple, turning her face aside. The click of the hammer locking back sent a shiver up her spine. She stopped struggling against her bonds. She looked at the sky out the shattered windows, at dark clouds rushing past.

It was all bullshit, she thought. All that stuff about having one's life replay at the very last moment. There wasn't time for that. There wasn't even time to say goodbye.

The pistol roared in her ear.

15

Godfrey flinched when his mother lightly touched the back of his arm.

"I didn't mean to startle you," she said. "There's food set out in the other room. Come and eat with us."

"I can't eat. I'm not hungry," he said.

"Are you well?"

Godfrey shrugged.

Niramala put her hand to his forehead. "You don't feel warm," she told him. "You can skip this meal, but tomorrow things are going to return to normal. Everyone in the family eats together and at the same time. Do you understand?"

The boy nodded. And his mother left, closing the door behind her.

Godfrey turned his unfocused gaze back to the wall. He wasn't sick, but many things were confusing him. They were things he had to sort out by himself. His mother couldn't help. Even his father couldn't help. And he couldn't tell them what was wrong.

Neither of them had seen Vallu die.

Neither of them had watched, frozen in place,

helpless, while a friend was tortured to death. Godfrey had remained, though he knew he could do nothing. There had been too many Sinhalese attackers and they had worked too fast. Even though he had wanted with all his soul to run away, he had remained because he owed it to Vallu. Because someone had to be a witness.

Before Vallu's murder, he hadn't really understood what death was about. In the comics the bad guys died, sometimes even the good guys died, but every time he opened the magazine to the beginning they were alive again, good and bad. There was no similar way to rerun Vallu's life. And the harder he tried to remember the man's face or the sound of his voice, the less distinct the memory seemed.

Some things in comics still seemed true to him. There really were heroes in the world. The man with the white hair was one. He was afraid of nothing. He had saved them from the army, the police, the rioters.

Now there was no hero to protect the family. There was only Godfrey. And he was scared. He couldn't let it show because he didn't want his mother and his sisters to be more frightened than they already were.

He picked up the sawed-off shotgun, cycled the action and ejected a single red shell. He shoved it back into the magazine and ejected another. His father had never let him play with the gun. He had fired it only once and that had been with his father standing behind him, helping him hold it up. And absorbing most of the shock of the recoil. The gun was much lighter now, with its shortened barrel.

He laid it on its side on the mattress and paced off six feet. He dropped a pillow at that point, then went back and shouldered the gun. Six feet was very close. Close enough to see a man's eyes. Godfrey swallowed hard. He wondered if he would have the courage to pull the trigger face-to-face.

A pounding from the other room broke his train of thought.

The door to the back bedroom opened and his mother and sisters rushed in. "They're here," Niramala said. "The police are here!"

Godfrey had rehearsed their exit so many times in his mind that it came now as second nature to him. He pushed out the screen over the small window, then shoved the bed under it. "Up and through," he said, helping his mother stand on the mattress.

From the other end of the house there were shouts and screams.

"Quick!" he said, pushing Jenny, then Sheila, through the opening. He passed the shotgun and ammo bag out to his mother before climbing out the window himself.

The window looked onto a tiny deserted alley.

"Which way?" his mother said.

That, too, Godfrey had already figured out. He led his mother and sisters down the winding lane at a trot, taking the first left, then the first right, putting as much straight-line distance between them and the police as he could. He made the women pause for a moment and listened. Running feet were coming after them.

"We must keep moving," he told them. "If we stop again, they'll catch us. Run! Run!"

This time he took up the rear, putting his body and the shotgun between his mother and sisters and the police. When he wanted them to turn he yelled. He was leading them out of the Muslim ghetto, back into the riot-ravaged Pettah. It was familiar ground to him, but the maze of streets had been transformed by fire. It was no longer necessary to go to a corner to cross over to another street. Not when there were so many gutted buildings.

"Hurry!" he cried, goading them over piles of fallen brick and charred timbers. It hurt his heart to hear Jenny sobbing in terror as she ran, but there were worse things than being scared. And the worse things were gaining on them.

As they broke through into the next street, headlight beams swung around a distant corner, pinning them. Blue-and-white roof beacon flashing, siren wailing, the police minivan bore down on them.

Godfrey dashed ahead, skirting the high stucco wall that formed the rear border of the Hindu temple grounds. He shoved the back gate aside and ushered his mother and sisters into the garden. In the disappearing daylight, the statues and the carefully manicured shrubs took on threatening poses and seemed to conceal legions of rabid murderers. Godfrey didn't give the women or himself time to consider the potential hazards. He drove them in front of him, down the gravel path.

Be open, he prayed as they neared the garden's front gates.

They were more than open. They were on the ground, torn off their hinges. The temple, too, was a shambles. There was a fire-blackened bus inside the ground floor. There were no floors between it and the roof. All had collapsed. All was destroyed.

Disaster had hit the street in front as well. As they ran across it, Godfrey saw dozens of white Tamil flags of mourning hanging from window frames that no longer held glass. Heaps of half-burned rubbish cascaded from the open doorways of ruined homes and businesses. Personal belongings too mangled to be of interest to the mob were ground into the puddles of mud in the center of the road.

No matter what happened from now on, Godfrey thought as they rushed into the narrow alley that ran behind the street of the slaughterhouses, nothing was ever going to be the same in his country. Not ever.

Even the impossible stink of the abattoirs was subtly changed, mixed with the smell of quenched fires. Not the usual household garbage burning. Hope burning.

"Stop!" someone shouted at their backs.

They did not. They raced down the dogleg with strength born of desperation.

Godfrey frantically rattled a back gate. Then another. And another. All locked. Around the bend they had just passed, running feet were approaching. And farther off, tires squealed as a police van turned down the alley. He crashed the butt of the shotgun into the padlock. He swung with all his might. On the third blow the lock snapped. Godfrey tore it from the hasp and pushed. The gate creaked and resisted. He herded mother and sisters through the gap. He followed. As he shoved the gate closed, the minivan's headlights swept around the bend.

The slaughterhouse yard was filled with long evening shadows, but its prominent features were still visible. A tin-roofed porch ran the length of the rear of the main building. The porch also ran along the stuccoed brick walls that bordered the perimeter. Under the tin roof were rows of shelves. On the shelves a clutter of containers, rope and the encrusted tools of the trade. In one corner of the yard was a big pile of bones. Beside it was a heap of animal skins and great metal tubs of collected blood and offal. Intestines were strung like party decorations under the rafters of the U-shaped porch.

Godfrey pushed the women into the shadow beneath the tin roof and made them kneel behind a long work table. He heard the policemen shaking the locked gates. Then the minivan appeared, its bright beacon gliding along the top of the back wall, moving slower and slower until it stopped opposite the gate.

Beside him, Jenny made a tiny whimpering sound. Niramala reached out and clamped a hand over the girl's mouth. There could be no noise now. Not if they were to have any chance at all.

Godfrey crabwalked closer to the gate, hiding behind a wooden barrel brim full of rainwater and something putrid, again putting himself between his family and the danger. If the police checked the yard, they were sure to be caught. If he fired the gun, he was sure to be killed. It was getting so dark he could hardly see the gate. Voices drifted over the back wall. He recognized one of them. Sergeant Perara. Quietly, carefully he pushed off the shot-gun's safety.

He didn't need to see to know the situation was grave; he could hear. The gate creaked as it was slowly shoved back.

The boy swung the 12-gauge to his shoulder, pointing it in the direction of the sound. His hands trembled, but his resolve was unshakable. He knew in his heart it was better to die fighting, to struggle to the last heartbeat, than to meekly submit to the destroyers.

The comic books had taught him that.

Barrabas had taught him that.

Vallu had taught him that.

16

Bullets from the plantation house whizzed over Barrabas's head and plowed the turf behind him. He slammed the steel butt of the AK into the metal turret, ringing it like a bell. "Get the lead out!" he shouted to Beck and Lopez.

He dropped to a prone position and returned fire on the shooters crouched behind the big stucco urns and decorative brickwork of the veranda. With the Chinese assault rifle's selector switch on semiauto, he punched out careful single shots, trying to keep the gunmen's heads down.

Barrabas opened his mouth to yell again, but caught himself when he saw Beck and Lopez crawling out of the turret. They bellied down beside him.

"Had a cold one stuck in the tunnel," Lopez explained.

The muzzle-blast of Beck's AK slammed Barrabas's ear as the skinny guy raked the porch rail with lines of lead.

"That's the way. Keep 'em down," Barrabas told him, scrambling to his knees. "Keep 'em way down."

With that, the white-haired man charged the

veranda. Three long strides carried him halfway across the dead zone. Then, from an upper-story window, a submachine gun chattered, and it was suddenly raining bullets. As he swung the AK up, he thumbed the fire-selector switch to annihilate, and shot one-handed, holding only the weapon's pistol grip. Muzzle-climb. In this case it was just what the colonel ordered. Running full tilt toward and under his target, Barrabas had no time to adjust point of aim. His slugs stitched up the side of the building, from a foot below the window to a foot above the upper casement, shattering glass, shattering submachine gunner. As he hit the stairs leading up to the veranda something fell heavily to earth behind him, fell close enough for him to feel the rush of wind. The submachine gunner did not even groan on impact. He was already so much dead weight.

The mercs on the veranda realized they were about to be overrun and fought back hard, risking frontal fire from the MG emplacement to track Barrabas in their sights.

If they were counting on poor marksmanship from Lopez and Beck, it was a mistake. The kind no one gets to make twice.

Steel-cored slugs from the pair of AKs swept along the top of the porch rail, coring skulls, sending mercs and their gear skidding into the lawn furniture.

As Barrabas jumped the top step, the firing from the MG stopped abruptly. His SOBs didn't want to shoot him in the back. The two surviving mercs on the veranda had no such qualms. They rose as he ran past, trying to bring muzzles to bear. He punched the final round of the AK's clip into center chest of the man closest, then applied the sole of his canvas boot to the lock on the French doors leading into the house. The lock gave, as did the doors' beveled-glass windowpanes. Amid the tinkling shower of fragments, Barrabas ducked and pivoted, jerking his Hi-Power free of hip leather just as another flurry of shots sliced the air.

The remaining merc left his feet, lifted and propelled by the combined impact of a half dozen 120-grain slugs to sudden and final collision with the plantation house wall.

"Come on!" Barrabas shouted at Lopez and Beck, waving them on. Then he rushed into the mansion's main dining room, the cocked and unlocked Browning in his right fist.

Across the long room, a door was closing. Barrabas fired five quick shots through it, all at chest height. The 9mm parabellums bored through the hollow-core door and through what stood behind it. From across the room Barrabas heard the thud of meat hitting hardwood. From the sound, at least 190 pounds of it.

He holstered the Hi-Power and fed the AK a full mag. As he chambered a live round, Beck and Lopez burst into the dining room. Lopez had brought along something he'd found.

"Those guys already had it dismounted," Emilio

said, holding up the M-60. He was garlanded with 7.62mm belts, a three-quarters size Pancho Villa. "They were trying to get it turned on us. I figured we might need it."

"You're a touch light to handle that from the hip," Barrabas told him.

"If I start to come off the floor, Beck'll jump on my back. Won't you, Nate?"

Nate was at the door Barrabas had ventilated. He opened it a crack, peeked out, then jerked back fast. A hail of bullets gnawed at the wood where his head had been. "There's four or five of them hiding behind a staircase at the end of the hall," he said. "They've got position on us."

"Bullshit," Lopez said. "Here, let me show ya." He adjusted the belts so they would feed smoothly from floor to shoulders to M-60, then kicked the door open and hopped out into the hall. He started shooting even before he was all the way out of the room, knocking a painting off the wall, gouging holes in the floral-print wallpaper. By the time his feet hit the hallway floor, he was really wailing.

The M-60 had a well-earned reputation for "making things happen." It certainly made things happen to the mercs hiding behind the staircase. First, though, it made things happen to the staircase. As the machine gun roared, its feed belts sliding like live snakes over Lopez's shoulders a foot at a time into the ravening breech, its heavy slugs disintegrated the mercs' cover. Then it did the same to them.

Bodies backstepped and boogied, dancing against their will—puppets of pain.

Lopez cha-chaed, too, his whole body vibrating, legs shaking, knees knocking, but he kept it up until the staircase was reduced to a pile of wood chips and the enemy to twitching heaps of gore.

Barrabas pushed past him and ran down the hallway. He had to find Erika. He had to find her fast.

As he reached the bend in the corridor, there was a momentary lull in the shooting. An instant of perfect stillness.

It was broken by a single shot, the loud report of a short-barreled revolver.

The sound of an execution.

"No!" the white-haired man snarled. "God-damnit, no!"

"PICK IT UP, NANOS!" Billy Two yelled at the Greek's broad back. "Pick it up or I'm gonna run you down!"

"Up yours," Nanos wheezed over his shoulder. The body builder was sprinting flat out, pedal to the metal.

Billy Two could no longer see O'Toole's red head of hair bobbing in the lead. The stocky Irishman had quickly pulled away from Nanos and was somewhere on the jungle trail ahead, somewhere between them and the intense small-arms fire raging from the direction of the plantation house.

"It's that young stuff!" Billy Two hollered. "Do in an old guy every time!"

"How the fuck...would you know?" Nanos shouted back between gasps. "You've never...had a...date...that wasn't...on Medicare!"

"Tell me about it! I ain't even breathing hard."

"Hole-ee crap!" Nanos groaned, as both kick and wind deserted him.

Billy Two wasn't feeling so good, either. Queasy as well as overheated, the sweat squirting out of his skin. As if his whole body was about to cramp up. No way would he admit that to the Greek, though.

."All those pretty muscles and no go," he said. "What the hell good are they?"

Nanos couldn't answer. At that moment he would've gladly traded three inches of upper-arm circumference for a single eight-minute mile.

When they broke through the bush line and into the rubber-tree groves, Billy Two cut around his old buddy, turned on the speed and passed him with apparent ease. As he swept by, the Indian asked, "Want me to call you a cab?"

"Hit...a...tree," the Greek rasped back.

Billy Two could see O'Toole now, way ahead. He slowed down a little and tried to recover his breathing rhythm. The price for his burst of speed, his one-upping the Greek, was a hell of a side stitch. It had been worth it, though. Nanos in lust he was used to; it was the guy's normal condition. Semipermanent heat twelve months a year, length of daylight, ambient air temperature notwithstanding. But Billy Two was damned sick and tired of Nanos in love. The guy was no fun anymore. A tight and tanned bottom and a pair of pink-tipped et ceteras had turned one of the Western World's most highly decorated couch lizards into a character from an Ingmar Bergman film.

"What the hell kept you?" Liam demanded as Billy jogged up to the entrance to the covered trench.

The Indian jerked a thumb over his shoulder. "Stuck behind a slow truck."

"Jesus, is Alex runnin' or walkin'? From here I can't tell."

"I think what he's doin' is hurtin'."

"Pulled muscle?"

Billy Two grinned. "Yeah, I guess you could call it that. More of an overly pulled muscle, if you want to get technical."

From where they knelt, they could see the plantation house, its mercenary defenders shooting from the veranda and the rest of the SOBs returning fire, bullet for bullet, from the front of the MG position.

"We don't have time to wait for him. He can catch up. Let's go."

The Irishman slithered through the tunnel opening and disappeared. Billy followed with difficulty. His shoulders were at least a size too big for the hole. He lost some skin doing it, but he kept up with O'Toole and exited at the other end right on his heels.

The colonel and the others were nowhere in sight but their handiwork was everywhere. Bodies. Lots and lots of bodies. As Billy looked back across the mine field for Nanos, the bursts of small-arms autofire from inside the house were suddenly smothered by the horrendous clatter of an M-60.

"We'll take out the front left MG first," O'Toole told him. "I'll go through the tunnel, you go overland."

"Gotcha," Billy said. As he dashed to the corner of the building, flame winked at him from their intended target and machine-gun slugs clawed the dirt a step behind. He dived for cover, grunting as the ground came up and slammed the AK into his gut. "Nanos, where the hell are you?" he muttered, rolling to his feet, putting his back to the wall.

There were more than a couple of major bitches to the situation. First, the machine-gun team had moved their weapon to the top of the turret so they could direct fire along the side of the mansion. Second, he had no backup, thanks to the Greek. Third, if he went overland, as O'Toole had ordered, he would be handing Son Ny's mercs six foot six inches of target. He decided to potshot a bit before he played the human bullet trap.

Billy Two switched the AK to his left shoulder and knelt. Though normally a right-handed rifleman, he could shoot southpaw when the terrain demanded it. It was a survival trick he had picked up many wars ago. He took a deep breath, let it out, then swung around the corner of the building, lining up cylindrical post, tangent notch and the head of the guy behind the M-60. He squeezed and the assault rifle bucked. As he rode the recoil wave back on target, the machine gun opened up. The Indian fired five quick single shots as 7.62mm slugs swept across the grass toward him. On the fourth, the machine gunner's head disappeared from above the turret. And the shooting stopped.

Billy Two didn't think. He moved. He thumbed the AK to automatic and rushed the emplacement, zigging, zagging, shooting from the hip, trying to cross the finish line before the M-60 could be re-manned.

He didn't make it. A head popped up behind the enemy weapon. Running full tilt, he couldn't direct accurate fire at the emplacement. The M-60 roared, chewing up the turf ten feet in front of him.

"Oh, shit," he said, diving for the dirt. "Shit!"

Then came the tight string of whacks from behind, bullets whining over his back from the other direction. The machine gunner swung the M-60 barrel up to meet the new threat, but too slow. Too late. He cartwheeled out from behind the turret and landed in a thrashing pile on the grass.

As Billy Two twisted around, a powerfully built figure rose from a shooting crouch at the building's corner. Even in the dim light, the Indian could see the wide grin smeared over Alex Nanos's face.

"Slow and steady wins the big one every time!" the Greek shouted at him. "You ought to give it a try in the sack, too. A change of place from the famous Native American wham-bam."

I'm never gonna hear the end of this, Billy Two told himself as he hurried for the front left corner of the house. Not in a million years.

As the Indian neared his goal, a flurry of autofire gunshots boomed from within the nearest MG turret. O'Toole had finally made his presence known. When Billy Two peeked out around the corner of the mansion, he did so at ankle height, on all fours, his head down and his behind high. The response from the remaining MG position was immediate, if off target. A hail of NATO-caliber lead gnawed at the stone facing five feet above his head, chewing downward in a swift, deadly arc.

He ducked back.

"What's the holdup?" Nanos asked as he joined him.

"The mercs manning the right front emplacement have moved their M-60 out from the armor, too. They've got this corner of the building nailed."

"Not for long," the Greek said, nodding at the turret across from them.

O'Toole wriggled from the bunker entrance and, with the cover and concealment of the metal housing between him and the surviving machine gun, managed to get behind the deserted M-60. His teeth bared in a half grimace, half grin, the red-haired man savaged the mercenary position with autofire.

"That's our cue," Nanos said, bolting around the corner ahead of the Indian.

Billy Two was forced to bring up the rear. Running behind the madly juking Greek, he could not shoot without risking his pal's life. Nanos and O'Toole were doing more than enough full-auto unloading to pick up the slack. As they dashed the length of the mansion's front, charging for the emplacement, the mind-numbing chatter of gunfire was matched by the frenetic clanging of lead on steel.

When they were fifteen feet from the turret, the M-60 behind them shut off. A head popped up on the far side of the machine gun dead ahead.

Billy Two growled a warning as Nanos fired. Two bright casings jumped from the AK's ejection port and the would-be machine gunner jumped backward, arms spread wide, crashing to the grass with a pair of ragged holes torn through his heart.

A second merc rose from cover, his CAR-15 held hip high.

Nanos swung his autorifle onto the new target and pulled the trigger. Nothing happened. He had run the 30-round mag down to zero. "Hole-ee shit!" he groaned.

Billy Two was ready. As the Greek turned sharply, dropping to one knee, dropping out of the line of fire, he stroked his AK's trigger. The 5-round burst plucked at the fabric of the merc's fatigue shirt, climbing up his chest to his head. It did not pluck at his head; it emptied it.

While Nanos hurriedly reloaded, Billy Two rounded the turret, poking the muzzle of his Chicom assault rifle into the ventilation hole. Nobody at home.

He looked up in time to see the third member of the MG team come rushing out of the bunker entryway, rushing straight for the kneeling Greek with a commando dagger in hand.

Nanos couldn't see the guy because his back was turned and Billy Two couldn't shoot because at the range of ten feet the steel-cored Russian slugs wouldn't stop with just one torso. He vaulted the MG turret at the same moment the merc made contact with Nanos, locking a forearm around his bull neck, sweeping the stiletto's long razor edge up for a quick left-right slash across his throat.

Before Nanos could cry out, before the merc could bring the blade to bear, Billy Two closed the gap, jamming the snout of the AK between the Greek's back and his attacker's front. He pinned the trigger, using the barrel and stock as a lever to turn the bullet-spewing muzzle into the merc's guts.

Son Ny's soldier clung to Nanos's back as point-blank Russian shorts pulped his intestines. His screams cut through the din of autofire. Then he dropped away, limp, spinal cord severed, to the grass.

"Jesus, Billy, you fried my back," Nanos said, looking over one massive shoulder at the charred ruin of his shirt.

"You can get over a few powder burns. Not a cut throat."

"Yeah, you're right. Thanks."

"This makes us even."

"Even?"

"Yeah, for your saving my ass before."

"Sure, whatever's right," the Greek told him. Then he grinned. "But you've got to admit it, I did a neater job for you than you did for me. Technique versus brute force."

"Don't say it," Billy Two warned him.

"You ought to try it in the sack."

"I knew you were going to say it."

BARRABAS RAGED down the hallway, kicking in doors.

He met no opposition until he was almost at the end of the corridor. He gave a door the boot and as it swung in, gunfire swung out, sizzling over his right shoulder and slamming into the opposite wall. Barrabas waded into the room, his AK bucking as he fed lines of lead into the top of an overturned desk, the hurriedly assembled cover for a pair of mercs. Bullets gouged mahogany, boring holes through veneer, through hardwood, through the concealed soldiers of Son Ny.

Only two more of the major general's mercenaries had the misfortune to cross Barrabas's path. They died in a clip-emptying barrage of Russian shorts that caught them flat-footed, weapons pointing the wrong way. They turned and twisted under the hail of lead, spinning into the ground as their legs crumpled under them.

When he finally broke down the right door and found Erika, his heart froze. She was slumped in the heavy chair she was tied to. He ran to her and gently lifted her face. There was no wound, front or back. But she was very pale. Her eyes opened.

For a second they were full of terror, then she recognized him. "Heiss," she said. "He put a gun to my head. He pulled the trigger. I thought I was dead."

"It's going to be okay."

"What about Gunther and T.M.? In Colombo, the taxi...."

"They're fine, both of them. Erika, I need to know about Heiss."

"He said something to me after he fired. A message for you, he said. He told me to tell you, 'Some other time.'"

Outside the house a car started up, engine bellowing.

"Not if I can help it," Barrabas said, dashing for the window.

The Mercedes was already rolling across the yard, onto the dirt track. There were two heads inside. And one hanging over the back bumper. The merc trying to hitch a ride wasn't having much luck. Son Ny wasn't stopping for anybody.

"Get 'em!" Barrabas shouted at Liam, Nanos and Billy Two, who stood below at the two front MG positions. He brought his own weapon up and dumped thirty rounds in nothing flat. He hit the car all right. He even hit the guy clinging to the trunk lid. But he didn't stop the car. Neither did the SOBs. By the time they got an M-60 on target, the Mercedes was disappearing between the trees that bracketed the road to freedom.

Lopez and Beck rushed into the library.

"All the mercs are dead, Colonel," Lopez said.

"Help her, then follow me," Barrabas told them, feeding his AK a fresh mag and sprinting for the door. He ran for the group of vehicles parked beside the mansion, found a pickup truck with the keys in the ignition, cranked it up and jammed it in gear. Fishtailing wildly on the grass, he wound the engine to the destruct point, then shifted into second and flipped on the headlights.

He had to catch them. And kill them.

He couldn't trust Jessup to do the job alone.

SON NY LAUGHED, high-pitched and frantic, as he skidded the big Mercedes out of the clearing and onto the dirt road. The g-force of the high-speed turn flattened Heiss against the passenger door. When the car straightened out he jerked down his seat belt and locked it. Even with high beams blazing, the track ahead was nothing but a blur.

"Slow down, you asshole!" Heiss snarled over the engine's howl, over the furious slithering of branches against the sides of the car.

Son Ny did not respond. He was hunched over the wheel, concentrating with everything he had. The mirrored sunglasses lay discarded on the dash. For once the man's all-consuming vanity had taken a back seat to something—survival.

"If you crack up, they'll catch us for sure!" Heiss shouted.

"I won't crack up," the major general said out of the corner of his mouth. "I know this road. I know every turn and switchback. I've been practicing this little trip for weeks."

"You'd better hope to God you're a better driver than you are a general."

"What the hell's that supposed to mean?"

Heiss raised his left hand. In it was the .38 Smith & Wesson snub-nose. "It means if you louse up, I'm going to blow your fucking head off."

"We're coming up on the ambush site."

"Slow down!"

They came up on the kill zone, the bluff, faster than either of them expected. The easy curve at fifty-plus miles per hour opened onto a newly created dead end. The overturned Taunus lay with its under-carriage toward them, angled and positioned so there was no way around.

Son Ny slammed the Mercedes into the smaller car's rear axle, veered off and ran straight into the soft dirt of the bluff. Everything and everyone came to a sudden and complete halt.

When Heiss woke up, an instant after impact, he looked out of a crazed windshield blanketed with dirt. Son Ny was already bailing out of the driver's seat. "You stupid son of a bitch!" Heiss snarled, scrambling out the passenger side and bringing his gun up.

Before he could find his target, headlights flashed on, blinding him. They were no more than twenty feet away.

"Move and you're dead," a voice from the dark-ness drawled.

17

Godfrey heard the policemen slipping through the open gate. He couldn't see them at all. He tried to count each as they stepped in and couldn't do that, either. There were too many of them and they were too close together. All the boy could do was hold his breath and pray for a miracle.

A violent rustling from the opposite side of the yard broke the terrible silence. It was punctuated by a gasp of surprise and a growled oath. Then a flashlight winked on, its hard white beam locking onto the big pile of bones.

It shuddered and squirmed as if alive.

Rats.

One hundred. Two hundred. A thousand. It was impossible to tell how many. They were on the bones, in among the bones, peeking out with angry red eyes. They all reacted to the danger at the same moment, squealing and scrambling for better cover, scampering in all directions at once.

The boy held the shotgun aimed a foot above the source of the flashlight beam. The target was too far away. More like twenty feet instead of six. He had to wait, to stay calm. He had to let them come closer or, even better, go away.

Some of the rats could not run. They were dying, having eaten the poison bait left out for them. They staggered and fell as they tried to flee. Some did not even get that far. They toppled down the stack of bones, landing on their backs or their sides, little legs kicking. Maybe, in their tiny brains, they thought they were running.

Godfrey ducked as a flashlight beam swept over the front of a barrel he was hiding behind.

A muffled cry erupted from the darkness at his back. The cry was Jenny's. Godfrey realized with sinking heart what had happened, what had brought about the disaster. The rats! They had run right over his mother and sisters.

The human noise brought an instantaneous response from the police.

"Get a light over there, quick!" someone directly in front of him said.

Godfrey heard the footsteps and committed himself to the only course of action he had. Mother, have the sense to run when I shoot, he thought as he stood up from behind the barrel. When the light flashed on, it was almost on top of him. By reflex, he pointed; by reflex, he pulled the shotgun's trigger.

In the bright strobe of the muzzle-flash, Godfrey beheld the agonized grimace of the Sinhalese policeman as he was blown off his feet. In the same fraction of a second the recoil hit him. It hit him much harder than he thought possible. Even though his feet were firmly planted and the weapon snugged hard against his shoulder, the savage kick knocked him backward, and he stumbled over some low, unseen object in the dark.

Before he could regain his feet, a dozen flashlights were on him. Then someone tore the shotgun from his grasp. Someone else put a foot on his chest.

"It's just a boy," one of the Sinhalese cops said.

"Look what the boy did to Dahanayake," Sergeant Perara said, shining his light on a huddled form on the ground.

Godfrey saw, too. In the middle of the man's chest was a great, gaping hole from which glistening fluids poured. The boy was instantly, rackingly sick.

"Hey, Sergeant, look what we've got over here," another policeman said. "More Tamil terrorists."

Niramala, Sheila and Jenny were huddled together, spotlighted against the cluttered shelves and trapped under the sights of a half-dozen Sterling submachine guns.

Perara stepped up to the Amirthalingam women, putting his light in their faces. "These terrorists, I recognize," he said. "I've been looking for them ever since the riots. Pretty ones, aren't they?"

The semicircle of Sinhalese police grunted their approval.

Only one of them was still concerned with official procedure. His voice came from the rear of the group. "We should arrest them all and take them in for questioning."

"What do we need to question them for?" another cop asked.

"Yeah, we already know what they did. They killed a policeman."

"In front of ten witnesses."

"Still, if we take the women back to the station and...."

"That isn't the kind of interrogation I had in mind," Perara told them. "The one I was considering was more informal. More like a private talk. Just us and them. Say, inside the building there."

"No!" Niramala said. "No, leave us alone! We've done you no harm!"

"That's right, your son has done all the harm. But you're about to make up for it by doing us some good," the sergeant said, squatting down and laying his hand on Jenny's thigh.

Niramala struck out with her nails, raking Perara's cheek, making him pull back from the girl.

"For that, you're going to get something very special once we're inside. I promise," he told her, straightening up. Almost as an afterthought, he backhanded her across the face.

His mother's cry of pain was more than Godfrey could take. "You're a coward!" he shouted. "You're all cowards!"

The sergeant put his light on the boy who lay on the ground pinned under the boot of another policeman. "Did you say something, terrorist?"

"They've done nothing. You've got no right...."

Perara crossed the ground in three strides, picking up momentum as he did so.

Godfrey saw the boot coming at his head but there was nothing he could do about it.

Everything went white, then black.

WHEN T.M. FINALLY ARRIVED IN COLOMBO it was nearly dark. He drove straight to the home of his Muslim friends. Even before he knocked on the door, he knew something was terribly wrong. The door had been forced open, its lock broken. When he gave the door a push, it swung inward.

He was met by the hysterical woman of the house.

"T.M.! The police came!" she cried. "Niramala and the children went out the back window—"

"How long ago?!"

"Ten minutes, maybe fifteen," she told him. "The police—they broke down the door and ran after them."

"Which way?"

"I don't know. They went down the alley behind our house."

T.M. turned away without another word. He knew where Godfrey was going to try to take his mother and sisters. That was more than the police could know. He jumped back in the car and cut a squealing U-turn.

The Tamil searched in panic, racing up and down the alleys and side streets, looking for signs of his family or signs of the police who were after them. He found nothing. Saw nothing. It was as if the earth had swallowed them up.

When he reached the temple, he stopped the car in front and got out. He reasoned that if his son hadn't been able to make it back to the warehouse because of the pursuit, he might have taken the women there for refuge. He called softly into the gutted shell of a building. And received no reply. He called again, louder.

Something moved. Not in the temple, but up the street, between a light post and the wall that bordered the temple garden.

A body propped against the wall slumped over on its side.

T.M. ran, his heart in his throat, blinded by his own worst fears. He thought it was Godfrey, murdered by the police and dumped in the gutter.

It was not Godfrey. It was a grown man, his lips and chin stained with red. T.M. bent over to see if he was alive and smelled arrack. The man was dead, all right. Dead drunk. Passed out on the profits of his looting. His face was smeared with the juice of the betel nut, not blood.

As he straightened up, T.M. heard another sound. A faint, shrill cry that sent a shiver up his back. It was Niramala. She was close. And she was in pain.

He raced back to the rubble inside the temple and grabbed a two-and-a-half-foot length of unburned two-by-four, then crossed the street on the run, heading for the alley of the slaughterhouses. Inside his head there was no room for fear, no room for reason; it was packed with wall-to-wall rage.

As he neared the bend in the alley, he could see the flashing blue-and-white glow of the police van's roof beacon reflected on the wall opposite and in the overflowing gutter. He slowed to a walk and stopped to peer around the bend. The minivan was parked on the left next to the wall. A lone policeman leaned against the van's rear doors, smoking a cigarette.

T.M. paused only an instant to lower the two-by-four out of sight along his thigh, then continued on, walking briskly around the bend.

The moment he stepped into view, the policeman straightened up a little, shifting his Sterling submachine gun on its shoulder strap so the pistol grip was within easy reach. He didn't throw away the cigarette, however.

When T.M. was fifteen feet away, the cop raised an open hand for him to stop. His other hand was busy tapping the ash from the butt. If the Tamil had any doubts as to what he was going to do at that moment, a second desperate cry from over the wall put an end to them.

The unexpected sound distracted the cop for a fraction of a second. Long enough for T.M. to take a two-handed grip on the hunk of hardwood and start his swing. He was not playing for the sacrifice; it was home run all the way.

The two-by-four thunked solidly against the man's temple, sending a shiver up T.M.'s arms all the way to his shoulders. It would have been a triple in any other ball park. In this one, there was no place for the cop's head to go. It slammed back into the sheet metal of the van's rear door, concaving it. As the cop bounced forward, hat flying, his knees buckled. Somehow on the way down he caught himself and started up again, rising slowly from the half crouch he had dropped to.

T.M. swung again, only harder, this time overhead and down, groaning from the effort as he put every ounce of his weight behind the swing. He delivered a pile driver of a blow that no human being could recover from. The Sinhalese slipped to the ground beside the van's back bumper and fell into immediate and violent convulsions.

T.M. dropped the two-by-four and lifted the Sterling and its sling strap free of the man's quivering shoulders. He stepped around to the side of the van and, in the light of the beacon, located the submachine gun's selective-fire switch. With some effort he forced it over to the full-auto position. Then he gave the weapon's actuator handle a pull. A live 9mm round popped out of the ejection port; a new round was chambered. The staggered box magazine held thirty-two more. With the Sterling ready to rip, T.M. slipped through the open gate into the slaughterhouse yard.

18

A smile spread across Walker Jessup's meaty face as the roar of a turbo-charged engine grew louder and more distinct by the second. The vermin were fleeing the plantation and, in the process, racing right into his sights. He squeezed behind the steering wheel of the Datsun, leaving the driver door in the fully open position. While he unlimbered his Combat Colt with his right hand, he reached up with his left and shut off the overhead courtesy light. He drew his feet up inside the car, exposing as little of himself to fire as possible. Jessup wasn't all that happy about using an imported subcompact for cover. He would've felt more comfortable with a '54 Buick between himself and destiny. The Datsun was engineered for giving MPGs, not for taking FMJs—full metal jackets. He braced his body against the car's doorpost, thumbed down the customized automatic's wide combat safety and sighted between open door and jamb.

The dark Mercedes jumped into view with a sudden glare of headlights, slamming into the undercarriage of the overturned Taunus, caroming off to the right and doing a head-on into the side of the bluff. On impact the 450 SEL's rear wheels hopped five feet in the air; its nose, buried under a half ton of avalanching dirt, went exactly nowhere.

Just like in the movies.

Jessup waited until he heard movement from the vehicle, then flicked on the Datsun's headlights, catching two targets as they piled out of the luxury wreck. He gripped the Combat Colt with both hands, his forearms braced on his knees.

His patience had paid off.

"Move and you're dead!" he told Heiss and Son Ny.

From where he sat, with rock-steady position, he had his pick of targets. He could have killed both before either took a step.

"Drop the gun, Heiss," he said. "Drop it where I can see it and move around the car real slow. Son Ny, you stay where you are. Right where you are. And keep your hands away from the shoulder holster."

The major general slumped back against the driver door, holding his fingers to his forehead. He was bleeding from a nasty gash over his right eyebrow.

Heiss let the snub-nose fall to the dirt and joined Son Ny.

"OK, now you, Major General," Jessup said. "Take the gun out and drop it on the ground."

The Vietnamese drew his nickel-plated .45 with extreme care and tossed it off to his left.

"Hands on top of your heads," Jessup told them, and when they complied, he extricated himself from the subcompact's front seat, keeping his weapon trained on them. He moved alongside the front fender, stopping well back of the wash of the headlights.

"Let me go," Son Ny said, in a voice shrill with panic. He lowered his hand and revealed a cheek bathed in glistening blood. "Let me go and you can have anything you want. Money. Name the amount and it's yours. Or drugs. Whatever you want. We can make a deal."

"You've got nothing I want," Jessup said. "I've already been paid for this job. For once, Major General, you're going to face justice. You're staying here until the man with the white hair shows up. Tonight he's the judge. He's also jury and executioner."

Son Ny glanced over at the darkness to his left, outside the perimeter of the headlight beams, darkness that was the jungle.

"Don't even consider it," Jessup told him. "If you even think run, I'm going to blow your kneecaps off."

Actually, the Texan was ready to do a lot more than that at the slightest provocation. Jessup had no liking for the role of executioner, but in Son Ny's case he was prepared to put aside personal preference. Some men deserved to die. The major general had deserved to die for a long time.

Heiss was another one who needed killing. But it wouldn't be tonight.

"You can go, Heiss," Jessup said. "The keys are in the ignition of this car. Take it."

Heiss didn't move.

"You can't let him go and make me stay!" Son Ny declared. "Why, this whole operation was his idea. It was all for his vengeance against Barrabas. I only went along with him for the sake of our friendship!"

"I said leave, Heiss," Jessup repeated.

"I don't understand. Why are you doing this? Who are you working for?"

"The CIA wants you out of this alive. They didn't list their reasons. And I didn't ask. I'm just performing a service in return for future goodwill. You know how the procedure works, I'm sure."

"There's something familiar about your voice," Heiss said. "I know you from the agency days, don't I?"

"You knew of me," Jessup answered, holding the pistol aimed between the two men at midchest height. "I never associated with dirt bags."

Another vehicle was coming down the track toward them, its engine howling.

"Go, Heiss," Jessup said. "And do it now. I won't put my butt on the line to save you from Barrabas. If he catches you, that's your problem."

The smile on Heiss's face as he hurried by, so confident, so smug, almost made Jessup change his mind.

Almost.

Without a word of goodbye to his old and doomed friend, Son Ny, Karl Heiss cranked up the Datsun, slashed a frantic K-turn and sped away.

Jessup didn't watch the taillights disappear. He was too busy watching Son Ny. With the headlights of the Datsun gone, his target was dim at best. The fat man moved closer.

The louder the engine roar from the direction of the plantation, the more goosey the Vietnamese became.

And he started talking a mile a minute.

It was not a good sign.

"There must be something you want," Son Ny said desperately. "I can get you anything. Anything and everything. Who would ever have to know if you let me get away, too? In the confusion of battle, accidents can happen. Regrettable mistakes can be made."

"I would know," Jessup told him, shifting his grip on the Combat Colt.

Son Ny instantly switched his point of attack.

"Do you really think I'm going to keep quiet when Barrabas gets here?"

"What are you talking about?"

"Do you think I won't tell him that you let Heiss get away? That you helped him get away?"

"I thought you were smarter than that," Jessup said. "Remember, I've got the gun. If I don't want you to say anything to Barrabas, I can make sure you don't."

"You don't care if he knows?"

"I don't care if you tell him. There's a difference. You, he's never going to believe."

Son Ny glanced over to his left, to the black wall

of bush, to the invisible spot where he had thrown his weapon.

Jessup knew it was going to happen. He knew the major general was going to make a break. The talk was just distraction while he figured the angles. The Texan could almost hear the gears whirring in Son Ny's head. The Vietnamese thought he stood a better chance of survival going up against a .45 auto bare-handed at a range of ten feet than in facing the wrath of Nile Barrabas. Or maybe he figured he'd get a cleaner death from Mr. Colt.

It was too dark to see Son Ny's eyes. His sockets were hidden in deep shadow. That made Jessup very uncomfortable. The eyes were always a dead giveaway; they invariably blinked, darted, shifted before a sudden movement. The much smaller, much quicker man was only a few feet from the jungle, from concealment and freedom. He was also canny enough to use any advantage he had, or thought he had, to the fullest.

Son Ny moved.

And Jessup fired, suckered by a head fake, a juke worthy of an all-pro halfback.

In the hard light of the muzzle-flash, the Texan saw the rear passenger windows of the Mercedes disintegrate and Son Ny dive the other way, toward his gun.

"Shit!" Jessup growled, swinging the Colt around, firing again at the sound of a body hitting the dirt.

The cordite strobe told all: something bright and

shiny flashed in Son Ny's hands. The pimp gun. The major general had recovered his weapon.

The Combat Colt barked two, three, four times as Son Ny rolled for the front of the upturned Taunus. The last shot wrung a shriek of pain from the darkness.

Then a finger of flame winked back at Jessup. Something collided with his right shoulder. Something with enough foot pounds behind it to stagger the huge man and knock him sideways. He tried to raise his pistol to get off another shot, but his whole arm was numb to the fingertips.

Jessup shifted the Colt to his left hand and ran at the spot Son Ny had fired from. He wasn't going to let the bastard get away.

As the Texan rounded the front of the Taunus, headlights blazed on the dirt track in front of him, illuminating the crash scene and the escaping Vietnamese. Son Ny froze against the back bumper of the Mercedes, pinned in the glare.

Jessup went rigid, too.

It all happened so fast there was no time to react.

The driver of the pickup swerved to the right without braking. Swerved right for Son Ny.

The major general got one wild shot off before impact.

Then the scream of steel on steel, of shattering glass and plastic drowned out everything.

The pickup hit the Mercedes's rear end square on, folding it up like an accordion. Son Ny was caught in the middle. And literally sliced in half.

His torso slid up over the Mercedes's back window and onto its roof. His lower body remained trapped below the bumper of the pickup.

The truck's surviving headlamp spotlighted the grisly aftermath through rising clouds of dust.

Where a .45 auto had failed, an '82 Dodge had succeeded.

Jessup clamped gun and gun hand against his wounded shoulder. The pickup's driver door shrieked as it was wrenched open from the inside. Barrabas stepped down from the cab, his AK in front of him.

Now came the hard part.

19

T.M. moved among the shadows along the inside of the wall. He could see the rectangle of light from the open rear door of the slaughterhouse. He could also see the single policeman who stood watch outside. The man was as relaxed as his counterpart in the alley had been. He had his back to the yard and the gate he was supposed to be guarding. Framed by the doorway and the yellow light from within, he stared into the building with rapt interest.

More cries ripped the air. High-pitched and frantic. And they were followed abruptly by a chorus of raucous male laughter. The uniformed goons were delighting in his daughters' humiliation and terror. The sounds drove T.M. insane with fury.

T.M. skirted the shadows under the tin-roofed porch, low and quick, like a cat stalking its prey. Soundlessly, he stepped up behind the guard. The man had his Sterling submachine gun draped carelessly around his neck by the sling strap. The weapon hung behind his right arm, muzzle pointing at the ground.

There was more laughter from inside. Whatever the joke was about, it was now even funnier because this time the guard joined in, too, rocking back and forth on his heels as he chuckled.

The Tamil reached up, crossing his wrists, grabbing hold of the submachine gun's sling. The guard was still laughing when T.M. jerked the strap tight around his neck, cutting off wind and chuckle in the same instant, pulling him backward, out of the light and into the shadows.

Unable to cry out and alert the others, the policeman struggled violently, trying to dig his fingers in under the edge of the garrote, bending and twisting at the waist to throw his attacker off balance and off his back.

T.M. hung on stubbornly to the larger man, riding him like a rodeo star as they staggered backward together. Four or five steps, then the Tamil crashed into something solid. It caught him in the middle of his back. The cop realized he had his assailant pinned and pistoned his legs, trying desperately to gain leverage.

T.M. could feel the stronger man gaining on him. He couldn't twist the garrote tight enough and still maintain control of the cop's body. As he was ground into the hard rim of the thing behind him, fluid from it splashed all down his back and legs.

Timing his move with the guard's frenzied bobbing motion, T.M. twisted out from against the big barrel. Then he let the man's own momentum carry the two of them around. With a superhuman effort, he thrust the man's head and shoulders down into the overflowing barrel.

The policeman extended his arms to stop himself from going in. He could not get a grip on the slippery barrel and he plunged down into the liquid, arms and all.

T.M. threw all his weight on the cop's back and shoulders, clinging to the barrel rim with one hand while he held the garrote tight under the surface with the other. The man's kicking crescendoed. Then dwindled. It was only then that T.M. permitted himself to breathe. Only then that he smelled the contents of the barrel.

Not water.

Blood.

Rancid, putrid blood.

He pulled the slick, dripping corpse from the drum, laid it on its back and unwrapped the Sterling's webbed strap from its neck. The gun was not wet, but the strap was saturated. He shoved the fireselector button to automatic and again made sure a live round was chambered. He slung the backup gun over his arm, then moved forward cautiously into the light of the open doorway.

Inside the slaughterhouse, he saw the long butchering tables, littered with implements for the killing and dismembering of animals, and rows of meat hooks jutting from overhead beams.

What the Sinhalese officers found so amusing was not on the tables or suspended from the ceiling. It was laid out on the cement floor.

It was Jenny.

It was Sheila.

The clothes already torn from their bodies, the two girls were pinned, spread-eagled on the floor by policemen who knelt on their shoulders, their open thighs. Policemen already stripped from the waist down, naked and grinning, fully prepared to enjoy the spoils of the evening.

Niramala screamed again. A wail of outrage and horror.

On the other side of the room, one policeman held her arms twisted behind her back, while another gleefully shredded her dress.

T.M. saw his son, too. Godfrey was tied to a workbench, hands behind his back. His chin rested on his chest. He was unconscious. Or dead.

Jenny's shrill plea for mercy snapped T.M. out of his state of shock. With the Sterling's folded stock pulled tight to his shoulder, supporting the muzzle shroud with his left hand, he stepped through the doorway.

"Look out!" cried one of the men holding Jenny down. He pointed a finger at the entryway. "Look out!"

The policeman kneeling between the girl's legs, his bare buttocks angled toward the door, stopped what he was doing and glared over his shoulder.

It was Perara.

The sergeant's look of irritation vanished when he saw the horned snout of the Sterling aimed his way. "Get him!" Perara cried, diving away from the terrified girl.

Perhaps because of their panic at being caught

\,ith pants down and guns piled in a heap on a distant table, perhaps because of the storm of hormones pounding in their blood, the Sinhalese police were slow and clumsy, scrambling, fighting one another to get at their weapons.

Their confusion and panic allowed T.M. to work methodically, picking his targets with care, dispatching them with precision. The Sterling chugged against his shoulder as he punched seven 9mm slugs through the center of the nearest man's face.

Even as the first Sinhalese folded and dropped, T.M. pivoted, locking new targets between the prongs of the submachine gun's sights.

About half the men were headed for the weapons heap.

T.M. raked them with flanking fire, starting at their intended goal and working backward, the Sterling's trigger pinned. The first two Sinhalese public servants to reach the table reached it dead. T.M.'s sustained full-auto burst dealt them multiple chest and head hits, dropping them in midstride, sending them crashing face first into the table legs.

The rest of the policemen scattered as T.M. discarded the emptied submachine gun and unslung his backup. There was no way they could recover their weapons, no way they could get out the door without going through him. He turned on the men still holding his wife.

"Let her go," he said, his voice a guttural rasp.

The cops clutched at the woman with the ripped dress, using her as a shield.

T.M. wouldn't allow it. He charged the officers, feinting left then cutting right. They tried to keep the Tamil woman between themselves and the madman but it was impossible. Their efforts were not coordinated; they both pulled or pushed at the same time, negating the effect; and Niramala was fighting them all the while, trying to throw them off balance.

The Tamil jabbed his Sterling's muzzle into the exposed side of one of the men and ripped off a 3-round burst that went through and through, the exiting slugs whacking into the wall behind. As the wounded man fell screaming to his knees, his accomplice abandoned the living shield and sprinted for the door with everything he had.

T.M. swept the entire room navel high with autofire as he tracked the running target, chopping the man down from behind.

The Sterling came up empty.

Everybody in the room knew he was out of bullets.

The three surviving policemen stepped into the light, out of the shadows where they had been cowering. Their angry faces reflected a confidence that had been sorely lacking only moments before.

"We're going to hang you on one of those meat hooks up there," Perara said. "Give you a balcony seat while we finish what we started with the women...."

T.M. threw down the useless submachine gun and grabbed an ax from a nearby bench. Before

Perara and the other two could find weapons of their own, he rushed them, ax held high.

One of the men stood his ground, fumbling on the table for a long thin filet knife. He raised the blade, taking a bent-kneed fighting stance. T.M. ignored the razor edge, ignored the danger of being disemboweled and swung with everything he had, over head and down.

The heavy ax blade came through the policeman's guard as if it was made of tissue paper. T.M. hit what he was aiming at—the join of left arm and shoulder. The downward fall of the blade met resistance, but it was only momentary. Token. The filet knife clattered to the floor along with the arm and hand that still held it.

Tightly clutching his empty shoulder socket, the shrieking Sinhalese ran in circles—tight, crazy circles. Red splashed the floor, a pinwheel of blood.

The man wasn't worth another blow of the ax. He was already dead.

T.M. pursued Perara and the remaining cop around the room, trying to corner them. Though both had grabbed knives, they made no attempt to stand and use them. Neither one had any stomach for the fight now.

The Tamil put on a sudden burst of speed that caught the two Sinhalese by surprise. Perara went one way and the other man went down, stumbling over his own feet.

Before the man could get up, T.M. was on top of him with the ax, delivering a downward blow so powerful that it shattered the top of his skull, caving it in, spraying brains and gore in all directions.

T.M. had to use his foot to free the blade. By the time he managed it and looked up, Perara was halfway to the door, head down, legs pumping, bare buttocks jouncing. T.M. dashed after him, angling his run to cut the sergeant off before he reached the exit.

"No, please!" Perara howled, covering his head with his arms as T.M. closed the gap.

The Tamil swung the ax again, this time with the blunt edge down. His first blow caught the man on the forearm, knocking him sideways. His second was aimed at the ankles and clipped the feet out from under him. Perara sprawled on the concrete on his belly, less than a yard from the doorway.

He quickly rolled to his back, his face contorted, pale with shock.

T.M. was there to greet him, looming over him, the ax raised high. This time the bright edge was down.

"Don't! Don't!" he wailed, clutching at his shattered forearm, holding it over his head.

T.M. swung and the sergeant dodged. The ax head hit the floor with tremendous force, sparking on the concrete. Too much force. The handle splintered with a loud crack and the head jumped free, skittering off into the darkness of the yard.

Seeing his chance, the sergeant scrambled up and turned to make a break.

T.M. hit him with the ax handle. First one arm,

then the other. Sizzling blows that slammed the sergeant three feet to the right, three feet to the left. Blows that echoed like gunshots in the low-ceilinged room.

Perara ran anyway, out into the yard. He ran screaming at the top of his lungs. Screaming for help. Screaming for the police. Screaming murder.

T.M. tackled him from behind, bringing them both crashing to the dirt. The sergeant could no longer use his arms as they were both broken, but his vocal cords were still in fine shape.

He bellowed up into the face of the man who straddled him and held his shoulders pinned to the ground.

T.M. pressed both his hands against the screaming mouth, but he could not stop the terrible noise. Frantic to end the nightmare, to get his family to safety, he fumbled along the ground next to him for something, anything to kill Perara with.

A rock.

A stick.

A broken bottle.

What his fingers closed on was none of the above. It was soft, still warm, still feebly wriggling. T.M. crammed the dying rat into Perara's gaping mouth, crammed it head first, wedging it deep.

The sergeant went rigid under him, gagging, arching his back, then frantically shaking his head. T.M. jammed his palm hard against the rat's rear end, holding it firmly in place, grinding the back of Perara's head into the dirt.

Still the man thrashed; still the man screamed. Through his nose. High and shrill. Fingernails on a blackboard.

In a frenzy, T.M. smashed down with balled fists, raining blows on the rat's hindquarters, pounding it deeper, raining blows on the bridge of Perara's nose, pounding it flat. Cartilage crunched under the heel of T.M.'s hand, hot blood splattered his shirtfront and the screaming stopped.

The sergeant's remaining airway was closed.

In three minutes both rodents were dead.

20

Barrabas showed no interest in the two-part corpse he had just created. He walked away from the Mercedes and its new roof ornament without even a curious glance. His concern was for slime bags among the living.

The three-car pileup completely blocked the narrow road. There was no way he could get around the tangled wrecks without help. Tow chains would have to be rigged. Or the vehicles would have to be rammed off the track and into the bush.

"Where's Heiss?" he demanded of the fat man. Then he saw the blood trickling down Jessup's biceps, under the butt of the Colt .45 auto he gripped and held against it. "You shot?"

Jessup nodded.

"Who did it?" Barrabas asked as he examined the wound in the light of the sole surviving truck headlamp. It was from a single slug, a clean-through track only about an inch and a half under the blubber of his upper arm. It was hardly bleeding at all.

"The dead one over there. Hey, you know this thing hurts like shit."

"You'll live," Barrabas assured him. "Now what about Heiss?"

"Gone. Got away."

Barrabas squinted against the hard glow of the headlamp. The angled light cast shadows over half his face, undercutting cheekbones, brow, jawline. The expression in his eyes was icy cold, as was the tone of his voice. "How's that again?"

"He took off while I was chasing Son Ny," Jessup told him. "I couldn't run them both down. I had to make a choice. And I did."

"The wrong choice. Son Ny was a nothing. A nobody."

As Barrabas looked over Jessup's shoulder, the scowl that twisted his features deepened. "What happened to the Datsun?" he asked, staring into the fat man's eyes.

"He took it," Jessup said, then he changed the subject. "Erika—is she all right?"

"Heiss put a gun to her head and pulled the trigger. He aimed for the wall. It was supposed to scare the hell out of her and it did. For Heiss it was a joke. Fun and games." The white-haired man raised his AK level with the Texan's massive gut, thumbing the fire selector from safe to full-auto. "Jessup," he said, "tell me you didn't have anything to do with Heiss getting away. Make me believe it's the fucking gospel or I'm going to turn you and Son Ny into a pair of bookends."

Barrabas watched the fat man's face. Jessup wasn't afraid, he could tell that. But the discomfort etched in his eyes was the result of more than the flesh wound.

"You wanted some help fast," the Texan said. "I got it for you. You shouldn't be surprised if I had to make a deal to arrange it all."

"A deal? With who and for what?"

Jessup leaned against the side of the pickup. "I had to call in some favors with official channels. They weren't enough to cover the outlay. I had to throw Heiss in as well."

Barrabas said nothing.

"It was either him or Erika," Jessup went on. "I figured you'd prefer to save her life."

Again Barrabas searched the Texan's sweaty face. He couldn't tell if he was being fed gospel or garbage. As far as Barrabas was concerned, sneaky petes, active or semiretired, were liars by nature as well as profession. Instinctive, creative liars. The only thing he knew for a fact was that Karl Heiss was gone. And his initial judgment of Walker Jessup had been proved correct. The fat man could be trusted only as far as he could be shot-putted.

"If you're telling me the truth," the white-haired man said, "you did the right thing under the circumstances. You made the same choice I would have. If you're lying, pray to God I never find out." He lowered the AK.

"I'm not lying. My one burning ambition is to avoid becoming a bookend."

"You didn't say who I have to thank for all this."

"An official agency of the U.S. government. I can't tell you more than that."

"Don't get coy with me. We both know it's got to be the CIA. They're the only ones he had connections with. They're the only ones who could've engineered the transport and documentation of my guys so quickly. Why the hell would they want Heiss alive? He's been on their kill-on-sight list for years."

Jessup didn't respond.

Barrabas answered his own question. "A special mission, no doubt. Some piece of dirty work he's uniquely qualified for. I hate to think what that might be."

"You and me both," Jessup admitted.

"I also hate to think how stupid the CIA is to trust that scum ball again. You'd think they'd have learned their lesson in Vietnam."

"Maybe they don't trust him. Maybe that's what they can depend on."

Barrabas glared at the Texan. "Circles within fucking circles," he said. "That what I hate about you guys. Nothing is ever straightforward. The shortest distance between two points is always a curve."

Jessup smiled. "That's what makes life interesting."

"It also makes people dead."

The white-haired man stepped past Jessup and walked around the wrecked autos to the deserted road on the other side. He could only see a few feet into the darkness, but he could feel the track ahead with his mind. Feel it winding, weaving, then opening onto the Colombo road. From there a million different paths were possible. No one more likely than any other. The certain knowledge that pursuit was out of the question burned in Barrabas's guts like a slowly twisted knife.

Once again Karl Heiss had his freedom.

Once again the man had pulled off another miracle of survival. He was like a cockroach. Frozen. Starved. Sprayed with poison. And always coming back. Always hungry.

"Some other time" was the message Heiss had left with Erika. Words he wanted his old enemy to chew on for the duration. It was more than just a threat against Barrabas personally. As long as Heiss drew breath, there could be no safety for anyone or anything Barrabas loved.

The cockroach was a hardy creature, but it could be killed. Under a heel. With a stone. Squashed.

The white-haired man glared into the jungle darkness, his lips forming words only he and the night could hear.

"Sometime soon, Karl," he said.

21

Barrabas stood with his back braced against a forward bulkhead as the 727 taxied down the Colombo airport runway. He was surveying the handful of passengers that were the plane's only cargo.

"A bit bruised, eh, Colonel?" said O'Toole, who stood by his side.

Barrabas nodded. There were lots of bruises and lots of bandages. Jessup had one wing in a sling. Gunther and Godfrey were sporting matching white turbans. Erika had a gauze pad taped to the side of her face. Nanos was bare chested, wearing a compress strapped to the small of his back. Sheila and Jenny both had black eyes and Niramala a cut lip.

"It could have been a whole lot worse," he said, pushing away from the bulkhead and moving to his aisle seat beside Erika.

As he buckled his seat belt, she gave him a big smile.

"You look damn chipper, lady."

"Got reason to be. My friends are all safe, and they're going to stay that way."

Barrabas looked across the aisle at T.M. The Tamil was leaving the land of his forefathers, tak-

ing his family with him. He no longer had the luxury
of a choice in the matter. The violent deaths of so
many Sinhalese policemen were sure to be thoroughly investigated. Sooner or later, the Amirthalingams'
connection with Perara would be uncovered. There
was no question of T.M. and Godfrey coming forward and telling the truth, explaining to the
authorities that the killings had only been in self-
defense. No Sinhalese magistrate would have dared
let them go. Not with the mob still howling for Tamil
terrorist blood. The whole family would have been
fed to the Sri Lankan penal system, father and son
executed, mother and daughters imprisoned.

The 727 rolled to the white line painted on the
tarmac, stopped for a moment, its engines winding
louder and louder. Then the plane began to glide
forward, picking up speed in a mad rush. The
wheels left the ground with a bump and the jet
banked as it rose, giving Barrabas and Erika a view
of Colombo baking in the midday sun.

They had only been airborne a few seconds before
Gunther rose from the seat in front of them. His
head bandage was tipped at a jaunty angle, sprigs of
straight blond hair sticking out from between the
turns of gauze. He gave his sister and Barrabas a
wink, then leaned across the aisle to T.M., Godfrey
and Jenny. "What day is it, kid?" he asked the boy.

"Tuesday," Godfrey replied without hesitation.

"Naw, it's your birthday."

"My birthday isn't for three months."

"Shut up. It's your birthday. And in honor of the

occasion, the guys and me have arranged a little surprise. You do like fireworks, don't you?''

Godfrey looked at his father, who shrugged and shook his head. T.M. was as puzzled as his son.

''Sure I like fireworks,'' the boy said.

''That's what I thought,'' Gunther said. ''Hey, everybody, it's showtime! Everybody on the port side of the plane!''

The SOBs, Jessup, Barrabas and Erika all moved over.

''What about the time, Beck?'' Gunther asked.

''On the button,'' the little guy said. ''Fifteen seconds, give or take a couple.''

''Ladies and gentlemen,'' Gunther announced in a loud voice, ''may I direct your attention to the pier coming up. Watch the warehouse on the very end.''

''Gunther, that's—'' T.M. began.

His words were cut off by singing. Of a sort.

''Hap-py Birth-day to you. . . .''

Gunther and the SOBs belted out the first two bars of the song with enthusiasm, if not perfect agreement on the key.

On cue, the pilot dipped his wing, giving them all a direct downward view of the tan building.

A flash of intense red-orange enveloped the whole end of the pier, blowing out all four of the warehouse walls, obliterating the roof. The blast drove a circular shock wave across the surface of the water, a ring that grew wider and wider, more gigantic by the second, racing away from the central spire of gray-black smoke.

"Hap-py Birth-day to you. . . ."

The 727 headed out to sea, leaving the pyrotechnics behind.

The singing disintegrated into laughter.

"That was our warehouse!" T.M. said. "Our impounded warehouse!"

"Gunther, you didn't!" Erika said.

"Sure he did," Barrabas told her.

Beck clucked his tongue. "All those poor defenseless Sonys," he said, shaking his head.

Gunther was grinning from ear to ear. "Hey, kid, you just saw a million bucks blown to hell. Some birthday, huh?"

Godfrey nodded, his brown eyes huge and dancing with delight.

"Ask him what he's going to get you next year," Billy Two prompted.

"A picture of the faces of the Sinhalese bureaucrats when they get the double bad news," Emilio suggested.

"Double bad news?" T.M. said.

"Yeah," Lopez went on, "not only did they just lose their pension plan, but Dutchman broke even on the deal. He had the TVs insured all the time."

"Colonel, if you will forgive a suggestion," O'Toole said, a twinkle in his eye, "I think the moment is ripe. . . ."

Barrabas smiled in agreement. "Ladies, gentlemen," he said, gesturing toward the plane's lounge, "I am pleased to announce that the in-flight bar is now open. And that the CIA is buying."

JACK HILD

Though still an American citizen, Jack Hild no longer resides in the United States. His current whereabouts are unknown. No one associated with Gold Eagle Books has ever seen Jack, in person or in a photograph, or has ever spoken to him directly. His publishers deal with him through a European attorney-agent who forwards contracts, checks, fan mail. If you should ever meet Jack Hild—and are sure that it's really him—let us know. We'd like to hear about it!

SOBs

#4 GULAG WAR

by Jack Hild

MORE GREAT ACTION COMING SOON!

Nobody breaks *into* Siberia . . . except Nile Barrabas and his SOBs!

Their mission is to flatten one of the Soviet Union's most inhuman concentration camps, in order to free a very special prisoner. But the SOBs' incursion into the USSR is discovered early in the game. The Russians know the Americans are inside and play a waiting game to find out their target.

Somebody should have told Barrabas that *nobody* breaks into Siberia! Nobody, that is, in his right mind. . . .

Available soon wherever paperbacks are sold.

**Nile Barrabas and the
Soldiers of Barrabas are the**

SOBs

by Jack Hild

Nile Barrabas is a nervy son of a bitch who was the last
American soldier out of Vietnam and the first man into a
new kind of action. His warriors, called the Soldiers of
Barrabas, have one very simple ambition: to do what the
Marines can't or won't do. Join the Barrabas blitz! Each
book hits new heights—this is brawling at its best!

"Nile Barrabas is one tough SOB himself.... A wealth
of detail.... SOBs does the job!"
                                            —*West Coast Review of Books*

#1 The Barrabas Run   #3 Butchers of Eden
#2 The Plains of Fire   #4 Gulag War

Available or coming soon
wherever paperbacks are sold.

**GOLD
EAGLE**

HE'S EXPLOSIVE.
HE'S UNSTOPPABLE.
HE'S MACK BOLAN!

He learned his deadly skills in Vietnam...then put them to good use by destroying the Mafia in a blazing one-man war. Now **Mack Bolan** ventures further into the cold to take on his deadliest challenge yet—the KGB's worldwide terror machine.

Follow the lone warrior on his exciting new missions...and get ready for more nonstop action from his high-powered combat teams: **Able Team**—Bolan's famous Death Squad—battling urban savagery too brutal and volatile for regular law enforcement. And **Phoenix Force**—five extraordinary warriors handpicked by Bolan to fight the dirtiest of antiterrorist wars, blazing into even greater danger.

Fight alongside these three courageous forces for freedom in all-new action-packed novels! Travel to the gloomy depths of the cold Atlantic, the scorching sands of the Sahara, and the desolate Russian plains. You'll feel the pressure and excitement building page after page, with nonstop action that keeps you enthralled until the explosive conclusion!

Now you can have all the new Gold Eagle novels delivered right to your home!

You won't want to miss a single one of these exciting new action-adventures. And you don't have to! Just fill out and mail the card at right, and we'll enter your name in the Gold Eagle home subscription plan. You'll then receive four brand-new action-packed books in the Gold Eagle series every other month, delivered right to your home! You'll get two **Mack Bolan** novels, one **Able Team** book and one **Phoenix Force**. No need to worry about sellouts at the bookstore...you'll receive the latest books by mail as soon as they come off the presses. That's four enthralling action novels every other month, featuring all three of the exciting series included in the Gold Eagle library. Mail the card today to start your adventure.

FREE! Mack Bolan bumper sticker.

When we receive your card we'll send your four explosive Gold Eagle novels and, absolutely FREE, a Mack Bolan "Live Large" bumper sticker! This large, colorful bumper sticker will look great on your car, your bulletin board, or anywhere else you want people to know that you like to "live large." And you are under no obligation to buy anything—because your first four books come on a 10-day free trial! If you're not thrilled with these four exciting books, just return them to us and you'll owe nothing. The bumper sticker is yours to keep, FREE!

Don't miss a single one of these thrilling novels...mail the card now, while you're thinking about it. And get the Mack Bolan bumper sticker FREE as our gift!

BOLAN FIGHTS AGAINST ALL ODDS TO DEFEND FREEDOM.

Mail this coupon today!

Gold Eagle Reader Service, a division of Worldwide Library
In U.S.A.: 2504 W. Southern Avenue, Tempe, Arizona 85282
In Canada: P.O. Box 2800, Postal Station 'A', 5170 Yonge Street, Willowdale
Ont. M2N 5T5

FREE! MACK BOLAN BUMPER STICKER
when you join our home subscription plan.

YES, please send me my first four Gold Eagle novels, and include my FREE Mack Bolan
bumper sticker as a gift. These first four books are mine to examine free for 10 days. If I
am not entirely satisfied with these books, I will return them within 10 days and owe
nothing. If I decide to keep these novels, I will pay just $1.95 per book (total $7.80). I will
then receive the four new Gold Eagle novels every other month as soon as they come off
the presses, and will be billed the same low price of $7.80 per shipment. I understand that
each shipment will contain two Mack Bolan novels, one Able Team and one Phoenix
Force. There are no shipping and handling or any other hidden charges. I may cancel this
arrangement at any time and the bumper sticker is mine to keep as a FREE gift, even if I
do not buy any additional books.

NAME   (PLEASE PRINT)

ADDRESS   APT. NO

CITY   STATE/PROV.   ZIP/POSTAL CODE

Signature   (If under 18, parent or guardian must sign.)

This offer limited to one order per household. We reserve the right to exercise discretion in
granting membership. If price changes are necessary, you will be notified.

166-BPM-PAD

MB-SUB-

Offer expires March 31, 1985